Joseph S. Coyne

**Young Frank's Holidays**

Doings out of school

Joseph S. Coyne

**Young Frank's Holidays**
*Doings out of school*

ISBN/EAN: 9783337286927

Printed in Europe, USA, Canada, Australia, Japan

Cover: Foto ©Andreas Hilbeck / pixelio.de

More available books at **www.hansebooks.com**

p. 30.

THE HAPPY FAMILY.

# YOUNG FRANK'S HOLIDAYS,

OR

## Doings out of School.

## BY J. STIRLING COYNE.

ILLUSTRATED BY M'CONNELL.

LONDON:

ROUTLEDGE, WARNE, AND ROUTLEDGE,
FARRINGDON STREET.

NEW YORK: 56, WALKER STREET.

1860.

TO

## Young England

THIS VOLUME IS AFFECTIONATELY DEDICATED

BY

A Friend to Mirth without Mischief,

WHO WAS

ONCE A BOY HIMSELF.

# PIPPINS AND PIES.

## Prologue.

"Write me a prologue."
*Midsummer Night's Dream.*

"'Pippins and Pies!'—What an odd title!" exclaim some of my young readers—" What does it mean?" Well, I am not too proud to explain, if they will have the patience to listen to a short story, by way of prologue to what is to follow. One evening, in the month of March — never mind the year,—I was at the Paddington terminus of the Great Western Railway, seeing a friend off to Bristol by the mail-train, when my attention was attracted by a young girl, who was sitting on a bench near the door, crying bitterly. Otherwise there was nothing remarkable in her appearance; her dress was studiously plain; a brown merino gown, with a grey Tweed shawl of scanty dimensions closely pinned across her neck

B

and bosom, and an unpretending straw bonnet
tied under the chin with a blue ribbon, completed
her attire.  A gingham umbrella and a small
deal box were on the ground beside her.  I had
the curiosity to glance, as I passed, at the large
card — I may, indeed, say placard — pasted on
the cover of the carefully-corded box, which displayed in fair round characters the following
address :—

> Miss Martha Mims,
> *Passenger,*
> Newbury.

"Martha Mims!"—There was not a particle
of romance in the name, nor the slightest tinge of
sentiment about the girl.  This gave me courage
to address her :—still it was not without some
embarrassment that I stammered out—

"I beg pardon.  You appear distressed :—can
I be of any assistance to you?"

The girl withdrew her handkerchief from her
face, and looking earnestly up, discovered a set
of features neither remarkably handsome or regular, but full of intelligence.

"My pocket has been picked, sir," she replied,
in a half-startled deprecatory tone, as if she feared
being severely reprimanded for the fact.  "Indeed
it has ;—I could not help it.  I was in the crowd

trying to reach the place where they deliver the second-class tickets, when somebody stole my purse from my pocket, and dropped it empty beside where I was standing. See"—and she held out a very small green net purse, unconscious of a single coin, to demonstrate her loss. "I called, 'Stop thief!' but the people behind me only cried, 'Move on!' and a policeman, marked 'G. W. R. 16' on his collar, asked me if I knew the thief, which, of course, I did not; but I thought it was G. W. R.'s duty to stop him. Then I certainly did begin to cry. If it was wrong, I'm very sorry. Some persons said it was 'a pity,' and others said it was 'a shame,' and G. W. R. observed it was 'a bad job,'—which it is, indeed; for how am I to get down to Newbury without a penny in the world?—and it's no use going back to —— Square."

"You live, then, in —— Square?"

"I *did* live, sir, at No. 9,—Mr. Pickleberry's. I was NURSERY GOVERNESS there; but Mrs. Pickleberry has parted with me, and I was going down to my uncle's, near Newbury, but for this misfortune."

It required no great consideration, nor any extraordinary pecuniary sacrifice on my part, to pay for a second-class ticket for poor MARTHA MIMS, who could scarcely believe her senses when I slipped the card and a few shillings into her little

green purse, and desired her to hasten to the
platform, as the last bell for the train starting was
then ringing. She would have delayed, notwithstanding, to express her grateful acknowledgments,
had not the vigilant G.W.R. reminded her "if she
didn't want to be left behind, she had better take
her place at once," at the same time hurrying her
to the platform. I saw her for one moment,
smiling pleasantly, and nodding her green umbrella at me, as the door closed, and I lost sight
of MARTHA MIMS, as I fancied, for ever. You
shall, however, hear how we met again—Martha
and I—after a lapse of six years, as they say in
the play-bills, when the audience at a minor
theatre is politely requested to stretch the half-
dozen minutes between the acts, to as many years.
It happened this way. One day I was a passenger
in a Chelsea omnibus, going towards the Bank ;—
I say *towards* the Bank—not *to* it—lest any of
my readers should fall into the mistake of imagining I was going to receive my dividends there, which
was really not the case,—when we were hailed
in the Strand by a stout little woman carrying
a green umbrella and a huge bouquet, or, more
properly speaking, a fagot of flowers and ever-
greens, under shelter of which she advanced towards the vehicle, like Macduff's soldiers approaching Dunsinane behind their " leafy screens."
Scaling the step by a vigorous effort, the new-

comer completely filled up the doorway with her stout person, her *monstre* bouquet, and her green umbrella.

"Conductor, the omnibus is quite full," murmured a voice from behind the bouquet.

"No, ma'am; there's room on the left. Sit a little closer there on the left. All right!" cried the conductor. Bang went the door, and away started the omnibus with a jerk that threw the lady off her balance, and would have pitched her backwards against the door, had she not made a desperate clutch with her disengaged hand at the most prominent object within her reach, which happened to be the long nose of a tall man in green spectacles, who at that moment was indulging in a nap, and being wakened up by the violent compression on his nasal organ, sneezed loudly, and looked over his spectacles with that sort of comic amazement which Box exhibits in the farce when he discovers Cox's mutton-chop on the gridiron where he had just left his own bacon. Recovering herself by the momentary assistance of the sleeper's nose, the intruder endeavoured, in evident confusion, to make a movement in advance; steadying herself by her umbrella, which in her agitation she planted on the toe of a corpulent gentleman of gouty tendencies, who gave a yell of agony, accompanied by a plunge that shot the little woman into the

arms of his *vis-à-vis*, a thin upright man in the
garb of a Quaker, who quietly transferred his
burthen to a lawyer from Chancery-lane; the
lawyer in turn got rid of his incumbrance by a
dexterous conveyance which placed the lady on
my knees; her bouquet, by an involuntary effort
to recover herself, being thrust into the face of a
young gentleman, whose head grew out of the
stiffest and straightest of "all-rounders," and whose
upper lip was adorned with a delicate fawn-coloured
moustache.

"Good heavens!—stop!—conductor, stop!
I'm destroyed—stop, this moment, and let me
out," screamed the young man, whose cheek had
received some scratches from a branch of variegated
holly, which formed the centre of the floral fagot.

"I'm sure I'm very sorry," said the little
woman; "I didn't mean it, indeed; but one is
so knocked about in these omnibuses, that one
don't know where one is. I beg your pardon,
sir. I really wasn't conscious that I was sitting
on your knees. Bless me, if his cheek isn't bleed-
ing; stay, let me put my handkerchief to it;"
and drawing an ample bandana from her pocket,
she applied it to the injured cheek, amidst the
smothered laughter of the other passengers.

The young man struggled and remonstrated; but
the little woman, who felt she was only doing her
duty, held him fast, and lavished upon him the most

tender care, until the conductor, hearing himself
called in a feeble voice from the voluminous folds
of the bandana, stopped the omnibus, and permitted the terrified victim to escape from his well-
meaning persecutor.

"Dear me, did any one ever see the like?"
and the proprietor of the bouquet turned to appeal
to me, when, with a startling exclamation, she
relinquished both bouquet and umbrella, seized
my hand in hers, and shook it energetically.  I
imagine my countenance expressed something of
the surprise I felt at this unexpected demonstration of friendship, for she seemed a little abashed,
and letting go my hand, said,—

"I suppose you don't recollect me, sir?"

"I really do not."

"Can't you remember MARTHA MIMS, the
nursery governess, whom you so kindly assisted
six years ago at the Paddington railway-station?"

The whole scene was instantly recalled to my
memory :—but I could not sufficiently express my
surprise at the change which a few years had
wrought in her appearance.  The slight girl had
expanded into the full-blown matron, the once
pale cheek now glowed with ruddy health, and
the tearful eye beamed with happiness and good-
humour.

"Yes," said she, replying to my observation,
"I'm not much like what I was when you saw

me that evening at the station. I was a miserable
poor creature then, but I'm married and happy
now."

"I'm delighted to hear it, Martha."

"Ah, sir! but if you had not helped me, I
could not have gone down to Newbury; and then
I might never have met John Bigland, who had
come from Gloucestershire to visit his sister, who
lives close to my uncle's; and if we hadn't met
at church, he couldn't have taken a fancy to me,
and, after a while, have married me, and made me
the best husband in the county;—could he now?"

I agreed with my communicative little friend
that the contingency, under such circumstances,
was more than doubtful.

"I have so often wished to inform you of my
good fortune; but I had forgot to ask you for
your address that evening, and had no clue to find
you out. Would it be too great a favour, sir, to
request you to give me your card?"

"Certainly not, Mrs. Bigland;—there it is."

"Thank you, sir:—John will be so glad of this.
We have been in London these three days with
some friends who are going to Australia; poor
things! I never could abide the thought of a sea-
voyage myself, since I went to Gravesend once,
when I was, oh! so sick. I hear, sir, they have
gold so plentiful there that they rock the babies
in gold cradles—which I don't believe, though I

have four of them myself; the youngest, Johnny, the born image of his father, was cutting his blessed teeth when we came away, and naturally makes me anxious to get home again. Perhaps, sir, you have a family yourself, and can understand the feelings of a mother towards her babes; I have four of them, sir; and I don't wish to boast, but this I'm bound to say—that four sweeter, lovelier popsies, never blessed——"

"Anybody for the Bank?" cried the conductor, thrusting his head into the omnibus as it stopped at the junction of those immense thoroughfares which form the main arteries to the heart of the city. I do not use to moralise whenever an omnibus stops in the street; but I can never behold the restless multitude flushing the broad pavements at this spot without thinking, how many noble projects and sordid calculations — how many dreams of wealth and schemes of ambition—how many gloomy forebodings and sad retrospections—how many hopes and fears—how many generous impulses and jarring passions—are quickening in the tide which throbs unceasingly in those great channels of human life.

As my ride ended here, I quitted the omnibus, with another cordial shake of the hand from my brisk little friend, who repeatedly assured me that I should hear from her before long. And she kept her word; for in less than a week a railway-

carrier deposited at my door a hamper containing
a miscellaneous offering from John Bigland's
farm, consisting of a pair of ducks, a fat goose,
ditto turkey, a fine ham, a bottle of real ketchup,
a dozen of mince-pies, and a quantity of golden
pippins for the approaching Christmas. With
these was a letter from John himself, inviting me
down for a month's shooting to Gloucestershire;
and another from Martha, inclosing a little green
silk purse, containing the sum which, she said, she
had not forgotten she owed me, besides a debt of
gratitude which she could never repay.

All this was very agreeable, and very flattering,
as well; and as I surveyed my presents, I began
to entertain very exalted notions of human nature
in general. The ducks were pictures to look at!
"There is still something good in our species,"
said I, feeling the goose, which was certainly one
of the fattest of its race. "Gratitude is not
extinct in some hearts," I added, lifting up the
turkey, which could not have weighed less than
twelve pounds. "There are persons upon whom
an obligation is not thrown away," I exclaimed,
as I gazed upon that lovely ham. The pies, I
should have mentioned, were separately rolled in
what appeared to be the closely-written pages of
a school copy-book, from which I was disengaging
them with as much care as Dr. Pettigrew ever
bestowed in the development of an Egyptian

mummy, when, by accident, my eye fell on a line of the manuscript that attracted my attention, and led to a closer examination of the scattered pages, which, I soon discovered, formed a portion of a journal, or record of certain incidents in the life of my friend MARTHA MIMS. Having, with some trouble, collected the fragments, I found that they related to the occurrences of an eventful period in the life of poor Martha, during which her distresses and dilemmas were enough to exhaust the patience — even of a nursery governess. Having obtaind her consent to "do what I liked" with her confessions, I now present them to my readers without any further apology.

# CHAPTER I.

Introduction to the Nursery and its Inmates—A Practical System of Juvenile Education, and an Examination of the Pupils—A speaking Likeness of a highly intellectual and nervous Lady.

It was striking twelve before I had finished Miss Georgina's back-hair ; and, notwithstanding the resistance which this ornamental operation is certain to meet in the best-regulated nurseries, I succeeded in making two lovely French plaits, which hung down her back like a couple of bell-pulls. Miss Maria and Miss Arabella had been for some time engaged in one of the windows superintending the important business of a grand tea-party given by Arabella's doll, Miss Mowbray, to which Maria's doll, Mrs. Herbert, was invited. The arrival of the guests, and the ceremony of their introduction to an old bandbox, in which the company were assembled, and the profusion of compliments which passed on all sides during the festival, were, I must say, managed with wonderful ingenuity and decorum ;— indeed, if the dear little souls had been grown-up people, they could not have shown greater knowledge of the world than in the respect they paid to fashionable dolls. This deference to rank was, I fear, carried beyond the strict limits of etiquette, when Miss Mowbray ordered a plainly-dressed doll of the name of Smith to sit in the corner, as there was not room for her amongst the "ladies" at the tea-table. However, it is right, I suppose, that the juvenile mind should be early impressed with the necessity of preserving those distinctions, which Mrs. Pickleberry says are the "strata of society." I don't exactly know what she means by "strata," though I've an idea it is something in mathematics, which, as a nursery governess on ten pounds a year, exclusive of washing, I'm not expected to know anything about.

The proceedings of the party were watched with intense interest by little Alfred, the youngest of my charges, who being only four years old, and consequently not supposed to have arrived at years of discretion, was only allowed to sit on a hassock and look on at a respectful distance, though he occasionally manifested a strong desire to rush into the active management of the affair. Unfortunately for the serenity of the evening, both Maria and Arabella had occasion to leave the window for the purpose of conveying a young doll of rank to the *soirée* in a "Favourite" omnibus, when Alfred, watching his opportunity, plunged his hand into the bandbox, and happening to seize on poor Miss Mowbray — a delicate creature, formed of the purest wax,—thrust her into his mouth, and crunched her lovely features in an instant. The cruel demolition was witnessed by Arabella, who with a piercing shriek endeavoured to rescue the remains of the ill-fated Miss Mowbray, but only succeeded in snatching a pair of pink legs and feet furnished with red shoes from the remorseless jaws of the young cannibal, who, being thus forcibly robbed of a portion of his prey, set up a terrific howl, in which Maria—who always cries through sympathy—joined with all her powers of voice. It was fully half an hour before I could appease the storm sufficiently to commence my educational duties of the day by an examination of the three young ladies in that valuable work, *The Stepping-Stone to Knowledge,* whose miscellaneous contents I had strenuously laboured to transfer to their heads.

Beginning with Georgina — who being nine years of age ought to have known better, — I asked her, " What does the wool of sheep make ?" and what do you think she replied ?—" Mutton," —absolutely, " Mutton ! " I then inquired if she knew " what little insect makes honey ? " " Yes," said she, "the silkworm." " What articles are made from cotton ? " to which the answer was, " Buttons and small spoons." Thinking she might

be better versed in geography than natural history, I asked, " Who sailed round the world three
times ? " " The Archbishop of Canterbury," said
Georgina.   " No," interrupted Maria, smartly,
" it was Milton,"—an historical error which Arabella corrected by saying it was " William Rufus."
I was further informed that Christopher Columbus
wrote *Paradise Lost*,—that Dr. Johnson was accidentally killed by an arrow while hunting in the
New Forest,—that butter was made from malt and
hops,—and that tea came from Cornwall. Although
these answers were not strictly correct, I admit
they were all to be found in *The Stepping-Stone*,
so that my little pupils only misapplied them;
and I have some doubt if the fault was not partly
my own, that I did not put the questions after the
answers, a system which would have saved a great
deal of confusion and misunderstanding in our
studies.   I may here mention an instance of extraordinary precocity in Maria, who being a sly
young puss, puts such remarkable questions to
me while she is at her lessons, that I prefer send-
ing her to play to answering them.   It was only
this very afternoon, when I called her up to her
Scripture exercise, she looked demurely into my
face, and asked me if I could tell her " where
Moses was when the candle went out ? "   I declare, though I have a tolerable knowledge of
Scripture history, I was completely staggered by

the question,—for I was not aware at the time that Moses was in the dark; and I did not like to confess my ignorance to the little chit, who I saw was ready to laugh in my face; and I was thinking how I should shuffle out of the difficulty, when luckily Mrs. Pickleberry's bell rang for me. I never was so thankful for the summons in my life, as it allowed me to escape from Maria, who I dare say was glad enough to get back to her dolls; so, smoothing the bands of my hair,—for Mrs. Pickleberry don't tolerate curls—and putting a pin in my collar, I descended to the parlour, where she was seated after breakfast.

I may mention that Mrs. Pickleberry was a highly intellectual and nervous lady; uncommonly refined, and very fragile in texture—so fragile, indeed, that it was wonderful (as she said herself) how she sustained the severe shocks to which she was daily exposed from a rude, unsympathising world; though I never could understand what these shocks were, for she never rose till noon, and generally spent the greater part of the remainder of the day on a luxurious sofa, propped and wadded round,—like a curious piece of carved work,—with swan-down pillows and air cushions, reading the last fashionable novel by a roseate light admitted through pale geranium-coloured silk window-curtains. I must however do Mrs. Pickleberry the justice to say, although she was tyrannical and unreasonable, and turned off her servants regularly every month, which was the cause of her being called by them "the Cooks' Monthly Nurse," she always spoke in the softest and gentlest way possible, and never uttered an unkind word but with a smile that seemed like sunshine upon vinegar.

"Good morning, Miss Mims; how are my little angels this morning?" said she, with a languid smile, as I entered the room.

"Quite well, ma'am."

"I hope, my dear Miss Mims, you took the great trouble to give my sweet cherub Alfred the powder Doctor Chamomile sent for him?—but I need not ask, for I know you forgot it. Yes—yes—you forgot it, as you forget everything I tell you."

"Indeed, ma'am, I——"

"Now don't agitate me by telling me a false-hood about the matter; you know I abhor false-hoods, especially from a young person who undertakes the moral and intellectual culture of four tender plants, so dear to a mother's heart."

"I assure you, ma'am——"

"Pray be silent, Miss Mims; your loquacity is dreadfully distressing to my nerves. Give me that *flaçon*. Thank you. I was about to say something particular when you interrupted me; my memory has become so evanescent:- ah! yes,

I want you, as you must have a great deal
of spare time on your hands, to have the kindness to write a note for me to Miss Lafont, my
milliner, and tell her to call here to-morrow
at two."

"Yes, ma'am."

"And, perhaps, as you work so beautifully, you
would put the head on that Berlin-wool dog in
the frame."

"Yes, ma'am."

"And, my dear Miss Mims, if it be not tres-
passing too much on your leisure, will you cut
the leaves of the new novel I got this morning;
and give a Naples biscuit to my marmozet; and
pray tell Annette, my maid, I shall wear my white
lace and pink satin this evening; and at the same
time you may take the children a few turns in
the square. And oh! pray don't forget the song
you promised to copy for me; and—dear me,
what was it I wanted with you when I rang? I
remember now. My dear boy Frank is coming
home for the holidays to-morrow morning."

I thought I was expected to say something, so
I said, "Indeed, ma'am! I'm very glad."

"I don't require you to be glad, Miss Mims."

"I'm very sorry, ma'am——"

"Miss Mims, allow me to suggest the propriety
of your restraining your emotions, and attending
to what I say. Frank is to sleep in the blue

room, which I'll thank you to have made comfortable for him."

"Yes, ma'am."

"And you'll have the kindness to look after him, and keep him out of mischief while he remains here."

"Yes, ma'am."

"And, Miss Mims, I'll take it as a favour if you'll kindly prevent him from running up and down stairs in his horrid, thick-soled boots; and slamming the doors; and making altogether such a disturbance in the house as schoolboys usually do during those periodical vacations when they are permitted to distract their afflicted parents."

"Yes, ma'am."

"And, Miss Mims,—a—I believe that is all at present; but I dare say you'll forget every word I have uttered before you pass the door." And with a deep sigh, expressive of angelic resignation to her fate, she sank gently back amongst her pillows and closed her eyes, while I made my retreat to the nursery.

# CHAPTER II.

Master Frank Picklebury comes Home for the Holidays—
Creates a Sensation—And makes an Impression, not easily
removed, on Martha Mims—The Results of Early Education
displayed in the Happy Family.

IF ever there was a boy sent into this blessed
world to be the plague of every body he came
near, it was Master Frank Pickleberry. He was
a monkey from his cradle, and a perfect nuisance
before he was out of long-clothes. One of his
earliest efforts at fun, when quite a baby, was
to set up such a terrific scream in the middle of
the night, that the entire household, including
his half-frantic parents, would rush in their night
costumes to the nursery, certain that the house
was on fire, or, at least, that the dear child had
been seized with a fit; instead of which the
young rogue would be found, lying in his cot,
laughing at what he evidently considered a capital
hoax. Having once been nearly choked by a
brass button slipping into his throat, he ever after
used to amuse himself by giving such natural
imitations of strangulation at dinner, that I declare, I frequently did not know whether I should

faint on the spot, or give the alarm and run shrieking round the corner for a surgeon. I shall not, however, dwell on the miseries I endured with him while he remained in my charge, which, I thank Heaven, only lasted till he was nine years of age, when his genius, disdaining the narrow limits of the nursery, began to find employment in the drawing-room; and, on one occasion, manifested itself by certain *striking* improvements in the mechanism of a costly *or molu* table-clock, which caused it to chime the twenty-four hours off at once in a prodigious hurry, and then to stand stock-still—the stubborn thing, as if no tickling could make it ever tick again. This experiment on the clock, however, determined Mr. and Mrs. Pickleberry to send Master Frank to a boarding-school, and about a week after, I had the pleasure of seeing him take his departure for Dr. Drone's scholastic establishment at Brighton. Three years he had spent at this school, returning home regularly at the Christmas, Easter, and Midsummer holidays, improving in health and advancing in mischief, if not in learning, every "half." It was, therefore, not without certain secret misgivings, such as may be supposed to disturb the tranquillity of that peaceful domestic animal, the cat, when the smallest of terrier dogs intrudes himself upon her society, that I heard stop at the door the cab

that conveyed Master Frank from the London
Bridge Station to the paternal roof. I, however,
hastened down to the hall to meet him; for I
*will* say, that with all his love of mischief, he
was not a bad boy at heart, and I was really delighted to see how tall and handsome he had
grown since last holidays.

"Hollo! here's Martha. How are you, Martha?
Isn't it jolly to be home again?" he shouted out
the moment he got sight of me on the stairs.
"Come, give me a kiss, Martha, and send these
things up to my room."

I rather hesitated, for I was considering whether
nursery governesses should leave off kissing pupils
of the opposite sex who had attained the age of
twelve years; but I had not time to determine
this delicate question, for Frank, taking my face
between his hands, saluted me briskly two or
three times, and then burst into a roar of laughter,
in which the cabman, who was carrying the last
of a pile of boxes into the hall, impudently joined.
I was mustering up a look of what strong writers
call withering indignation, with which I meant
to annihilate the cabman, when accidentally
glancing at my reflection in a chimney-glass in
the parlour, the door of which lay open, I perceived that Frank, when he placed his hands on
my cheeks, had left upon them two black daubs,
that at a short distance might have been taken

for a pair of luxuriant black whiskers. I could only scream a slight scream, and hiding my face in my apron, rush upstairs, and endeavour, by a severe scrubbing with soap and water, to remove the first impression which that good-for-nothing boy had made upon me.

I could not help wondering at the number of boxes of different sizes that Frank brought home with him, not to mention a large wicker cage containing a great solemn-looking owl, that bore a striking resemblance to the picture of that celebrated lord chancellor—was it Lord Bacon or Lord Eldon?—who was so long making up his mind upon every matter, that people thought he would never make up his mind to die. However, that don't much signify, as I was only going to observe I never saw such a strong family likeness as there was between that owl and the picture of the old chancellor, which Mr. Pickleberry, being a barrister, and expecting some of these days to be raised to the woolsack himself, had hung over the sideboard in the dining-room, in what he calls a favourable light, which was certainly very much needed, considering the unfavourable light in which lawyers are generally viewed. While I was admiring the features of the bird of wisdom, who sate sedately on his perch, opening and shutting his great round eyes at me, Master Frank came running up to the

nursery, after having gone through the cere-
monial of being hugged and kissed by every
member of the family, during which operation
he accidentally managed to tread on the tail of
*Bijou,* his mamma's pet lapdog, who was lying
on a velvet cushion near the fire. The compliment was acknowledged by a piteous howl from
the aggrieved brute, and responded to by a sympathetic scream from his mistress, who, snatching her darling to her bosom, cast a look at Frank
that warned him to escape as fast as possible from
the maternal storm which he saw was ready to
burst upon him.

I declare I could have boxed the impudent
monkey's ears soundly for the trick he had played
me, especially when, with a provokingly saucy
look, he pretended to brush up an imaginary pair
of whiskers on his own cheeks, and asked me if I
thought "these sort of things" became him. I
did not, however, give him the satisfaction of
appearing offended, but turned off the matter by
asking him what he had in the number of boxes
he had brought with him.

"The members of my ' Happy Family.' "

"Your happy family! I really don't know
what you mean."

"Why, have you never seen the ' Happy Family' in the large cage, kept by a man who
stands opposite the National Gallery in Trafalgar

Square? Haven't you seen the owl, and the cat, and the rat, and the mice, the pigeons, and sparrows, and guinea-pigs, all living comfortably and jolly together, contrary to their nature, which, you know, is to pitch into each other?"

I perfectly recollected having once formed one of a group of admiring spectators in front of the cage, and being highly amused at the impudence of the sparrow perching on the head of the old tabby cat, who did not move so much as a hair of his whiskers to resent the familiarity. I could not, indeed, forget the circumstance, for when I put my hand in my pocket for the purpose of presenting a trifle to the ingenious proprietor of the cage, I discovered that some curious investigator had displayed his natural instinct by picking my pocket of my purse and a silver thimble.

"Well," said Frank, "you know it's only hunger and habit makes the creatures devour each other; the cat would not eat a rat, nor the owl make a breakfast on an innocent field-mouse, if they hadn't been brought up to it, just as boys are brought up to beef and mutton; so I thought I'd try if I couldn't rear a Happy Family of my own."

"What an idea!"

"Oh! it's all right; I went regularly to work, and got a young owl out of the nest, and a kitten before its eyes were open, and fed them on bread and milk in a loft over the laundry at Doctor Drone's. As they never saw a rat, a mouse, or a sparrow in their lives, they can't know that they are their natural enemies."

"It's not likely they should."

"Very well, then we'll have the first grand meeting of the family after dinner. Crowther, and Dawson, and the rest of the chaps in our dormitory, wanted to have it down there some night after we had gone to bed; but I wouldn't, as I meant that you, and Georgey, and Maria, and Bella, and little Alf, should see it before anybody else."

Was not that kind of Frank?

What a happy dinner we had that day in the nursery! Frank, who had been taken by his mamma in the carriage to visit his two maiden aunts (the Misses Flathers, of Pembroke Cottages, Kensington), came back in high spirits; for his aunts, who doted on the boy, had "tipped" him a half-sovereign each, and stuffed him, inside and out, with sweetmeats and bonbons; besides which, he had persuaded Mrs. Pickleberry to give a juvenile party, to which Frank was to invite Jack Strangeways, who could walk on his hands nearly as well as his feet; and Bob Smart, who was *such* a jolly chap! and the three Bumpsteads, who whacked the three biggest boys in the school one morning; and Tom Taggart, who crowed better than any cock in the world, and could do the buzzing of a bluebottle, the sawing of a board, and the puffing of a railway engine, to the life. And they were to have the Joneses, and the Parkers—sisters and all, because they were such famous girls at acting charades,—and little Egerton Paley, because, poor fellow! his father was dead, and he had neither brother or sister to play with him, and he always looked so shy and sad.

I could have kissed the dear boy for the generous thought! and, from that moment, secretly forgave him the black whiskers.

Frank, I should have mentioned, had made out a programme, or list of amusements for the holidays, which, I remember, embraced nearly all the sights and exhibitions in London, and would have required about six months' hard labour to accomplish satisfactorily. It was, however, arranged that we should visit the Zoological Gardens on the following day; and, if time allowed, we were to run over the Tower, and through the Thames Tunnel; leave our cards with Gog and Magog at Guildhall; visit Madame Tussaud's wax-works on our way home; and, in the evening, go to see Buckstone, at the Haymarket, or take a peep at Astley's, where a splendid historic and cabalistic equestrian spectacle, called *The Phantom Steed of the Bosphorus; or, The Demon of the Drachen-*

*fels*, was performed every evening to highly-elec-
trified audiences.

Well, we certainly were, as I said, the merriest
little dinner-party I ever saw.   Frank told us his
best school-stories, at which we all laughed
heartily, especially when he gave his celebrated
imitation of Monsieur Cheville, the French master,
finding his lost spectacles in his soup-plate at
dinner, which I must say was very droll.   Our
gaiety, too, was greatly increased by the unexpected appearance of a nice dessert, and a bottle
of real British currant wine, which Mrs. Pickleberry
had ordered up to the nursery in compliment to
Master Frank, with a charge that I should not
allow the young ladies and gentlemen to indulge
too freely in the generous beverage.   During the
dessert Frank amused us with several conjuring
tricks and sleight-of-hand performances, one of
which I must mention, as it nearly cost little
Alfred his life.   It consisted in the exhibitor
visibly swallowing a spoon, and afterwards, when
required, extracting it from his ear or his eye.
Alfred, who had been attentively watching Frank,
thought the operation remarkably easy, and having retired to a corner of the room, commenced a
private rehearsal, to which my attention was attracted by an extraordinary gluck—gluck—gluck
noise, and turning round I saw the blessed child
nearly strangled, with a fiddle-pattern silver spoon

in his throat, all but the Pickleberry crest, two gherkins proper, with the motto, *" Not so Green as we Seem,"* which I fortunately got hold of, and pulling out the spoon, happily preserved him from being sat upon by twelve substantial tradesmen at a coroner's inquest.

After I had recovered a little from the shock, Master Frank began his preparations for the grand exhibition of his " Happy family," at which Mary the cook, and Sarah the housemaid, and Theodore Tunks the page, were invited " to assist," as the French say. When we were all seated in order on one side of the nursery, the exhibitor placed his large cage, containing the owl, on a table in the centre of the room. He next produced from one of the boxes a mild-looking cat, who suffered herself to be placed in the cage without any difficulty, and appeared to regard without much surprise her old feathered companion of the loft where she literally first saw the light; while the owl, opening his round grey eyes, recognised his friend puss, whom he received with a solemn wink. A hedgehog and a couple of guinea-pigs were then introduced to the cage, as was a full-grown frog, who displayed his agility by jumping clean over the cat's back, a liberty which she did not attempt to resent. The feat was enthusiastically applauded by the audience, who wished to *encore* it; but Frank had already added a blue rock pigeon to the Family, some of whom received the new-comer with considerable perturbation. The bird of wisdom raised the feathers of his neck, and elevated his brows; while puss, agitated by some profound emotion, assumed a decidedly hostile attitude towards the intruder, who appeared far from comfortable in his new society. There was, however, no infraction of the peace attempted, and Frank feeling confident of success, let loose half a dozen sooty-looking sparrows amongst the party, one of whom fluttered directly into the owl's eyes, who with a wild scream dropped from its perch upon the head of the cat, at the moment that Frank had introduced a pair of white and a pair of brown mice to the cage. The sharp claws of the owl fastening on the poll of the cat, caused that vindictive creature to attack, tooth and nail, the involuntary aggressor, who shrieking horribly and flapping his great wings, retreated to the furthest corner of the cage, where, finding one of the trembling mice, who had crept there for safety, he unceremoniously snapped up his victim and made a hasty meal of him. At the same moment an unlucky sparrow was sacrificed to the ferocious vengeance of the cat, who now dashed with glaring eyes at the sides of the cage, which being upset by the commotion, tumbled on the floor, and the large door in the top flying open, the ill-assorted family made a general retreat from their Happy

Home, amidst the screams of the terrified children, and Mary the cook, who, having a mortal horror of mice, had jumped upon a chair, and gathering her clothes tightly round her legs, expressed a determination not to quit that position during the remainder of her short life. As for Sarah the housemaid, she didn't much mind a mouse, but a frog was her abhorrence, and when she saw the hideous creature jumping directly towards her, she made no more ado, but went off into hysterics, of which, however, nobody took particular notice. Frank and Theodore the page exerted themselves manfully to allay our terrors, and fortunately succeeded in recovering all the fugitives, except the cat, which flew up the chimney like a demon; and one mouse, that Mary the cook declared had got amongst her clothes or somewhere about her; a delusion that Theodore could not remove, although he offered to make a strict search for the missing animal. At last quietness being restored, and the cause of this terrible disturbance removed, the cook was induced to descend from her post of safety, though she still insisted upon holding her petticoats screwed round her ankles—a disposition of these garments which gave the lower part of her figure something the appearance of a boy's peg-top. Sarah had also recovered by this time, and being assured that the frog had been permitted to take a harlequin's leap out of the

window into the street, descended with the cook
to the kitchen, escorted by the fearless page
Tunks, both greatly disgusted at Master Frank's
" ridick'lus nonsense, thinking that cats, and mice,
and howls, could live peaceable together—which
respectable Christians find uncommon hard to do."

# CHAPTER III.

A Domestic Conspiracy, which results in a Startling Discovery—
Teaching the Young Idea how to Smoke—A Morning Lecture
interrupted by a Terrific Descent from an Attic.

I FELT it my duty to give Frank a serious lecture upon his incautious conduct; and I must say
he seemed exceedingly penitent, and promised to
be more careful in future with his experiments;
but I thought I perceived a mischievous twinkle
in the corner of his eye which did not quite satisfy
me. The evening, however, passed over without
any remarkable occurrence, though I observed a
good deal of confidential whispering between the
two eldest girls and Frank, but without the most
remote suspicion of the dreadful conspiracy they
were engaged in. Let me hasten to its recital.

I got the three young ladies and little Alf to
bed about nine o'clock, rather earlier than usual;
for I wanted to have a comfortable read by myself
of Harrison Ainsworth's *Old St. Paul's*, which
Sarah the housemaid, who has used up three
circulating-libraries, recommended to me as the
" ghastliest book" that ever was written. I cannot

D

explain why it is that, being naturally tender-hearted and timorous, I should delight in stories of human torture and supernatural horror,—I, that would faint to see a chicken killed, can take a distressing pleasure in the details of an execution, or dwell with shuddering satisfaction on a description of the agonies of a poor wretch upon the rack. I never in my life dared to walk through a churchyard after dusk, yet I candidly confess I have a taste for charnel-house literature; and I had made up my mind to enjoy the harrowing scenes which the Great Plague of London afforded to the graphic novelist. Frank had retired to the blue bedchamber, and being left to myself, I snuffed my candles—commenced reading, and I need scarcely say was soon absorbed in the fearful story, devouring page after page, until I came to the scene where Chowles, the coffin-maker, and his associates are described carousing amongst the piled-up coffins in the vaults of St. Faith. The scene was so vividly painted by the narrator, that I laid down the book, and listened with palpitating heart, almost expecting to hear the shouts of the drunken wretches. All was silent, however, and I was about to resume my reading, when I thought I perceived a faint odour of tobacco-smoke. I sniffed incredulously, —it *was* tobacco. I could not be mistaken in the perfume that came strong and full upon my nose.

Somebody was smoking in the house. But who could it be? Mr. and Mrs. Pickleberry were gone to the Italian Opera to see Herr Formes or Charles Kean, or somebody of that sort, in the *Sonnambula,* and were not expected home till past twelve; so it naturally occurred to me that the young man who came every evening to run the scale with his walking-stick upon the area railings, had been invited to supper by the cook, and was indulging in a pipe of the fragrant weed after refreshment in the kitchen. To convince myself of the fact, I opened the nursery-door, and then distinctly perceived that the smell proceeded from some of the upper rooms, and not from the lower regions. Hastening upstairs in the dark, my first impulse was to look into the young ladies' room, and there I beheld a picture that I shall never forget.

In the middle of the room, planted on the carpet, with a red shawl twisted by way of a turban round his head, and his legs crossed, was Master Frank, smoking—*actually* smoking a cigar, while Georgina, Maria, and Arabella, were sitting on pillows and bolsters, in their night-dresses, striving to follow his example, with cigarettes;— even Alf had got a piece of twisted paper alight in his mouth, and was puffing away at it in his little cot with the gravity of a German professor. I declare I felt so shocked at the sight, that any one might have knocked me down with a feather. What on earth would Mrs. Pickleberry say if she could see what I saw? Nothing would have persuaded her that I had not taught her darlings to smoke, and I should have been dismissed the following day with a character of being addicted to cigars, and a strong suspicion of brandy-and-water. But what most vexed me was the coolness of Frank, who, instead of being ashamed of being detected in his clandestine doings, puffed a whirl of smoke in my face, and offering me his cigar, said,—

"Try a weed, Martha!"

"Master Frank, you ought to blush for yourself, and I don't know that I shall not inform your papa and mamma of your shocking conduct."

The three girls had thrown away their cigarettes in alarm, and retreated to their beds, where they lay as quiet as mice, with the clothes drawn over their heads; but little Alfred, with the natural impudence of his sex, continued puffing away at his bit of twisted paper, regardless of the indignation that must have been depicted in my countenance.

"Come, Martha," said Frank, in the wheedling tone that he could adopt when he wanted to smoothe out the creases of my ruffled temper; "come, Martha, don't be *waxy*—we were only doing a Turkish divan, as we do at school after

the masters go to bed. You won't tell,—say you
won't,—there's a good girl?"

"Well, 'pon my word, I don't know that I
ought not—however, this time I will not, if you
all promise not to do anything so wicked and so
dangerous any more."

"We'll never do so again, Martha," replied
Frank.

"We'll never do so again, Martha," murmured
three echoes from beneath the clothes in the three
beds.

Alfred said nothing, having dropped asleep with
the twisted paper in his mouth, and his little head
hanging over the side of his cot.

"Very well; give me that filthy cigar, till I
throw it in the fire; and go directly to bed,
Master Frank."

The cigar was reluctantly relinquished, and
the offender, making me a profound salaam in
the oriental fashion, threw a summerset, and
retired from the room by that peculiar mode of
progression practised by young gentlemen who
do what is called "the wheel" for the amusement of coach and omnibus passengers.

I had shocking dreams all that night. One
time I fancied that I was revelling with Chowles
and his crew in the vaults of St. Faith, drinking hot rack punch out of dead men's skulls,
and dancing in a skeleton quadrille, amongst

broken coffins, with the ghost of Sir Charles
Grandison for my partner; then I thought I
was suddenly transported to the harem of some
Eastern sultan or caliph, who politely presented
me with a magnificent hookah, and requested
me to join him in a friendly pipe, with a hint, if
I refused, that I should be complimented with the
order of "the sack," and be dropped for safe
keeping into the deepest part of the sea, which
washed the walls of his palace.  Glad I was
when the cheerful sun dispersed these horrid
fancies of the night, and called me from my bed
to praise and thank the great Fountain of light,
and truth, and happiness in this world.

As it had been arranged we were to visit the
Zoological Gardens to-day, I took some pains
to make myself smart for the occasion; I had
on my black silk gown, and a new Dunstable bonnet, trimmed with pale blue ribbon, and a little
bunch of something that looked like groundsel
stuck on one side of it.  Well, we were all in
high spirits, and the dear little children had
made a stock purse to buy cakes, and nuts,
and apples for the monkeys, bears, and other
animals in the garden.  They looked really beautiful—I mean the three young ladies, for little
Alf was to be left at home with Annette.  They
were so happy at the thought of escaping for
a few hours into the free air and sunshine,

from the monotonous confinement of the nursery, that I had enough to do to restrain their exuberant gaiety, and to keep them from tossing their hair out of curl, and making figures of themselves after I had taken such pains to put them out of hand as neat as dolls.

We were all ready, except Frank, who had been nearly an hour upstairs dressing himself, when I was summoned by Mrs. Pickleberry's bell to the parlour. She received me with the sweetest of smiles, and the slightest inclination of the head, motioning me at the same time to take a seat.

"You are going with the dear children to the Zoological Gardens to-day, Miss Mims :—their papa wishes to indulge Frank, and *I* don't object. But I must entreat you to be careful of the darlings ; serious accidents have happened to children through the negligence of young persons having the care of them. I'm perfectly convinced,—though they don't mention it in the papers,—that thousands of lovely innocents are annually drowned in the Serpentine, or kidnapped by gipsies, while their governesses are occupied in flirtations with young medical students, who smoke cigars and spend their time walking the parks when they should be walking the hospitals. Of course, I don't mean to speak personally, but,—you'll pardon me, Miss Mims,—

I have noticed a certain giddiness in your manner that I don't quite approve of. Young women in your station should think only of the precious charge intrusted to them, instead of trying to attract the attention of gentlemen when they go abroad——I don't mean to wound your feelings, Miss Mims—but you'll have the goodness to take that artificial flower out of your bonnet before you go out with *my* children."

She called my little bunch of groundsel an artificial flower! I replied as meekly as I could,—

"Certainly, ma'am, if you desire it."

"I *do* desire it; and may I request that in future your bonnet may not be of so very remarkable a shape? and if your parasol was brown instead of blue, it would be more suitable to your position in my family."

I felt the tears coming to my eyes, and a choking sensation in my throat; but Mrs. Pickleberry, without appearing to notice my agitation, proceeded with her quiet torture.—

"I assure you I speak solely for your own benefit, Miss Mims; for if you were good-looking—which candour compels me to say you are *not*—what could you expect, by this levity of conduct, but to fall—as many misguided young women have done?"

Mrs. Pickleberry's admonition was broken short by the apparition of a female figure tumbling over

and over through the air, apparently from one of
the top windows, into the back area. Mrs. Pickleberry gave a feeble scream, and sunk back on the
sofa as pale as death. I sate quite still myself,
without power to move or speak; for, although
I had only a momentary glance of the form as it
dropped past the window outside, I knew the
bright yellow shawl and the cherry-coloured ribbons of the bonnet were those of Mary, the cook;
and the thought flashed instantly upon my mind
that she had quarrelled with her sweetheart, and
had taken that way of being revenged upon him.

"Good heavens! Miss Mims," exclaimed Mrs.
Pickleberry, gradually reviving, "will you sit
there and see me expire without moving a finger?
Why don't you speak? Who—who is it?"

"I think it is Mary, the cook, ma'am; and I'm
afraid it's not an accident."

"How! has she dared to commit suicide in my
house? What on earth shall we do? I suppose
we shall have a coroner's inquest, and they'll
report it in the papers,—and—Miss Mims! will
you show the slightest sympathy for me, by——
What's that?"

The inquiry was caused by a shout of laughter,
proceeding from the lower part of the house, and
the voice of Frank on the landing, hallooing downstairs—"Mind how you carry her up; and don't
bang her head against the wall."

Opening the parlour door, I beheld Theodore Tunks coming upstairs, with the lifeless body of the cook thrown over his shoulder. Inexpressibly shocked at the sight, I retreated hastily, with terror depicted in my looks.

"Is it the body?" shrieked Mrs. Pickleberry, hiding her face in the cushions of the sofa.

"Oh, please mum," cried the page, following me into the room, with the hapless victim of misplaced affection still hanging, head downwards, on his shoulder; "please mum, it's only——"

"Wretch! begone this instant; take it away—take it to a surgeon's."

"You don't mean, mum, I'm to carry a bolster to a surgeon's?" replied Theodore, dropping his burthen with a soft plump upon the carpet.

"A bolster!" echoed Mrs. Pickleberry, examining the prostrate figure through her eyeglass.

"Yes, mum, a bolster that Master Frank dressed in some of cook's clothes, and pitched out of the attic window."

"It's all right, mamma," chimed in Frank, showing his mischievous face at the door; "it's only a lark, you know; but didn't it look the very image of Mary?"

The original herself now curtseyed into the room, looking very red and indignant at the perpetrator of the joke, and, muttering something about "monkeys," lifted up her representative

THE DUMMY.                    p. 42.

like a bundle of dirty clothes, and marched off in high dudgeon. I don't know how Frank and his mamma settled the matter, for I left them together in the parlour; but in less than ten minutes the culprit returned to the nursery with half a crown which he had managed to extract, along with a free pardon, from his indulgent parent.

# CHAPTER IV.

A Visit to the Zoological Gardens—Sentimental Stanzas by an Animal's Friend—Introduction to the Lions by a popular Exhibitor—Mr. Sam Jones and the Elephant—An unexpected Shower Bath, and a Family Group—Thoughts upon Monkeys, and Reflections upon Bonnets.

At length we started on our Zoological excursion; the three young ladies and myself in a cab, and Frank on the seat with the driver. It was a beautiful day; and the gardens, which looked lovely beyond description, were crowded with visitors, from the humble mechanic, his wife and children—making the most of their brief holiday, by the eagerness with which they rushed from place to place, poking their noses into untenanted cages, and exploring unthought-of corners,—to the fashionable loiterers from Belgravia, who sauntered apathetically through the gardens while their carriages were waiting for them at the gate. The green, velvetty grass-plats, mapped over with beds of rich flowers, exhaling delicious perfumes, almost tempted one to disregard the official

notice in great white letters on black boards
through the gardens, requesting visitors "not to
walk on the grass." Indeed, I had enough to do
to keep my little flock together, so delighted were
they with the novel scene. At one moment,
Maria, escaping from my side, would be scamper-
ing like a wild thing across the parterres, and,
while endeavouring to capture her, Arabella would
have disappeared down some bye-walk which she
hoped would lead directly to the monkeys, for
whose entertainment she had stuffed her pockets
full of nuts. It was in one of these digressions
from our party that Georgina picked up a neatly-
folded paper, which turned out to be a copy of
verses from a poet to a young lady, who had probably dropped it in the gardens. Whether the
poetry was meant to be serious or humorous I am
not quite certain; but I rather think, when the
writer composed his verses, he had in his mind
that sweet little poem of Shenstone's—wasn't it
Shenstone's?—beginning with—

> " I have found out a gift for my fair ;
>    I have found where the wood-pigeons breed ;
>  But let me the plunder forbear,
>    She will say 'twas a barbarous deed."

The original was a great favourite of mine—so
simple, so harmless, and so truly poetical as it is.
The imitation does not come near it in purity of
sentiment, though I grant there are some tender

lines in it, mingled with others of rather a jocund
character.   I copy them here—

### AN INVITATION TO THE ZOOLOGICAL GARDENS.

I have found out a gift for my fair—
   I have found where the rattlesnakes breed ;
I have peep'd down the pit of the bear,
   I have seen the old lion at feed.

I have heard the sweet cockatoo's song
   Make melody through the lone vale ;
I've watch'd all the summer day long
   The monkey who swings by his tail.

I have seen the rhinoceros play,—
   I have gazed on the stately racoon ;
And now, love, together we'll stray,
   To the cage of the blue-faced baboon.

You wish'd—I remember it well,—
   And I loved you the more for the wish,—
To witness the beautiful Pel-
   ican swallow the live little fish.

We'll have such a capital joke
   With the bear when he climbs up his pole ;
But observe, 'tis forbidden to poke
   The beasts with your pink parasol.

Then come, dearest, never say " Nay,"—
   We'll ride all the way in a 'bus ;
There's only a shilling to pay,
   To see the Hip-pó-pot-a-mus !

Frank, who had been several times to the Gardens, undertook to introduce us to the "lions,"
and other celebrities of the place, and to describe

their habits and peculiarities; which, I must say, he did in a very fluent manner, although I rather suspect his facts in natural history were, in a great measure, supplied by his own fertile and lively imagination.

"This yeare hanimal," said he,—assuming the tone and manner of the gentleman who travels about to country fairs with a "spotted Hinjin, a boa constricture, and two hinfant halligators," in a caravan,—"This yeare hanimal, ladies and gentlemen," pointing to a white bear enclosed in a deep den with a strong iron gate, "is called the Polar Bear because he was originally diskivered a sittin', like the lord chancellor, on the top of the North Pole by that galliant navigator John Parry, who sings those funny songs that perhaps you haven't heerd,—for which reason I pities you. The Eskimoo Hinjins hunts the Polar Bear by the light of the *roaring boreolis.*"

"The what, sir?" inquired a simple-looking old gentleman, in top-boots and a wide-brimmed hat, who had been listening attentively to him.

"The *roaring boreolis*, sir," said Frank, with a sly wink at me; "'tis a sort of candle, sir, very much used at the North Pole."

"A candle?"

"Yes, sir; the magnetic *dip*, they call it: they're going to light the House of Commons and the Thames Tunnel with it next week."

"Bless my soul! What will they do next? I
shall certainly stop in town to see it. I haven't
been in London these five-and-thirty years. Let
me see—is it five-and-thirty years?—Yes, it was
the very year I married Mrs. Jones. My name
is Jones; I don't care who knows it—Sam Jones,
and I've got as pretty a farm as any in Norfolk.
—But as I was saying:—when I came up to London from Beccles, five-and-thirty years ago, we
had a fast coach, called 'The Lightning,' that did
the journey in three days; and I recollect my
grandmother—who lived before my time, and had
old-fashioned notions—used to say it was a tempt-
ing-of Providence to travel at such an awful rate.
I wish my grandmother could have travelled with
me yesterday in the express train."

We were now opposite the cages of the large
feline animals. The old gentleman gazed through
his green spectacles in fearful admiration at
the old lion, who was looking with good-humoured
ferocity through the bars of his prison at the
crowd outside.

"Perhaps you're not aware, sir," said Frank,
"that noble animal is the original old British
lion brought over by William the Conqueror, and
who has for several centuries been fighting the
unicorn for the British crown? He is now retired
on a pension for long service from the Horse
Guards, and has his statue erected over the gate

of Northumberland House at Charing Cross, where you may see it any time you pass that way. That's the magnificent Bengal tiger, sir; and that's the beautiful leopard. It's a curious fact, there are exactly as many stripes on the tiger as there are spots on the leopard; and what makes it more remarkable is, that nobody has ever yet been able to count the one or the other."

"Dear me! really! Very extraordinary! But I'm rather anxious to see the elephant, which I'm given to understand is a very intelligent animal."

"Oh! a regular topper, sir—especially in gymnastics and rope-dancing; we'll go directly to him if you like."

Away we posted across the gardens to the elephant-house, only stopping once by the way at a pond on which a number of beautiful aquatic birds were disporting themselves according to their various tastes. There was the stately swan, with her arched neck and snowy plumage, floating gracefully upon the smooth waters; the beautiful sheldrake—the dear little Chinese ducks—and the whole family of foreign and native teal and widgeon—diving, splashing, darting here and there, and performing a succession of flip-flaps with a rapidity that would have astonished a clown in a pantomime. On the margin of the pond stood a party of philosophic cranes like

E

sentinels, upon those slender legs that seemed scarcely strong enough to bear a stout bluebottle, with their long bills resting on their breasts, contemplating the unbecoming frolics of their aquatic kindred, and wondering at the bad taste of people who could admire birds with ugly webbed feet and shovel bills. One genteel-looking white crane, who held his head on one side with a peculiarly pensive air, and whose pink legs were more slender and longer than any of the others, was pronounced by Georgina to be the living image of the very fair-haired young gentleman who sits in the pew next ours at church; and Frank would have it that there was a strong family likeness between the great buzzard and Mrs. Pickleberry's respected uncle, John Stubbs, Esquire, citizen and cordwainer, who for the last twenty years has been perseveringly eating his way up to the aldermanic dignity.

On we walked, very fast, by a winding path, past one of the aviaries, where the feathered tribes of every race and clime—peacocks, pheasants, turkeys, pigeons, guinea-fowls, partridges, magpies, daws, jays, and "all their relations, green, orange, and blue"—were chattering, cooing, crowing, and screaming in chorus; on through the tunnel, and by the long straight walk overlooking the Regent's Canal, on which we could see, through the thick foliage of the trees that skirted that side of the gardens, the heavily-laden barges moving lazily along.

As we approached the domicile of the elephant, we perceived that he was in the enclosure at the back of his habitation, where he had just been enjoying the luxury of a cool bath, and was now carefully rubbing himself dry with a wisp of straw which he held in his trunk.

"So that is the elephant," said Mr. Sam Jones, fixing his spectacles to have a clear view of him. "Wonderful animal! Never saw anything in my life like it."

The sagacious creature having completed his toilet, advanced to the barrier, outside which a crowd of curious admirers had collected, who amused themselves by treating him to biscuits and apples, which he dexterously seized and transferred to his mouth by means of his long, flexible trunk,—a feat that, on each repetition, was warmly applauded by the spectators.

I was aware of the many uses to which the elephant applies his trunk, but I had not an idea it was so generally employed by punsters as I find it to be. During the ten minutes we stood near his enclosure, I don't think there could be fewer than twice that number of puns made upon it by different individuals. Most of the perpetrators were mild-looking gents, who had got the ivory handles of their canes in their mouths; but I

was sorry to see some elderly respectable men—
with families, too,—who ought to know better,
lending themselves to a practice which, I am
credibly informed, is in some manner connected
with picking of pockets.    At all events I was glad
enough when we got out of the company of persons that I did not feel quite comfortable near.
I must, however, relate a remarkable circumstance that gave me a very high opinion of the
elephant's sagacity.   Frank had been for some
time offering it apples, and when it used to thrust
its long trunk through the railings to receive
the proffered fruit, he would suddenly with-
draw it.   At last the mischievous boy thought
it would be a capital joke to give the simple beast
a marble—of which he had a handful in his
pocket—instead of a nut.   Our new companion,
Jones, who mightily enjoyed the philosophic
stoicism of the elephant under his repeated dis-
appointments, volunteered to try this ingenious
trick upon him.   The creature took the marble
gently with his nasal finger, turned it round once
or twice, and then dropped it contemptuously on
the ground as a thing not worth regarding; but
I noticed a nervous sort of flapping of his huge
ears, and I thought his little eyes twinkled with
anything but friendly expression towards the old
gentleman, who was laughing heartily at the
success of his hoax.

JONES'S SHOWER BATH.                    p. 53.

From the elephant enclosure we sauntered on
to the giraffes—those really genteel-looking creatures,—and then looked in at the beautiful deer,
antelopes, and gnus, in this quarter of the garden;
after which we retraced our steps, intending to
visit the monkey-house, where Frank promised
us plenty of fun. Well, we had got as far as the
elephant-house, when the sagacious animal, who
had been apparently watching for our return,
suddenly discharged at least a bucketful of
muddy water from his trunk upon the head of
old Jones, who had stopped a moment behind us.
If I were to live a thousand years I don't think
I should ever forget the ridiculous figure the poor
man cut, with the water dripping in a circular
shower from the edges of his broad-brimmed hat,
like one of the fountains in Trafalgar Square;
while Frank screamed with laughter—and, I am
sorry to say, his rude behaviour was imitated by
the majority of those present, though they were
not aware that the ducking was richly merited by
the old gentleman for having tormented the un-
offending creature. Having somewhat recovered
his breath, which had been completely taken
away by his unexpected shower-bath, and dashing
the water from his eyes, the astounded Jones
glared around with a comic sort of amazement,
until, gradually comprehending what had happened, he started suddenly off at the top of his

speed, shouting murder with all the force of his
lungs, and was soon out of sight; though we
could trace the path he had taken by the trail of
water dripping from his clothes. I confess I could
not myself avoid joining in the laugh, when I saw
the poor man scudding desperately down the long
walk, to the inexpressible terror of several respectable old ladies and quiet parties, who trampled over
flower-borders and broke into forbidden places
to escape him.   One solemn gentleman, of the
*paterfamilias* pattern, who carried a short fat wife
under one arm and a cotton umbrella under the
other, with six chubby children in his wake, perceiving the strange figure of Jones rushing towards
them, and imagining him to be a lunatic broken
loose, endeavoured to avoid him by plunging down
the precipitous bank which overlooked the canal,
dragging with him his terrified partner and
shrieking little ones, one over the other, to the
bottom.

There they lay higgledy-piggledy, an undistin-
guishable mass of legs and arms, bonnets, hats,
and parasols, amongst which I could distinguish
the great cotton umbrella in a state of violent
excitement, and a pair of very remarkable legs,
that, by their proportions could only have be-
longed to the stout mother, kicking, with asto-
nishing energy, at nothing in particular, while a
general cheer from the juvenile spectators testified

to the delight with which they regarded the ludicrous situation of the family.

I tried to look uncommonly grave upon the business, and hurried my charge away to the monkey house, where a number of visitors were collected, watching the mischievous pranks and gambols of those little wretches, who jumped, and screamed, and chattered, and exhibited as much roguery and malice, and cunning and revenge, as if they had been made for the purpose of lowering man's pride, by showing him, in a miserable caricature of himself, the vices and meannesses that degrade his nature.

Although I have a strong dislike to monkeys generally, I was rather interested in a grave-looking one, with a blue nose, and a white ruff round his neck, like Lord Bacon, who sat in a corner of his cage, with his head resting pensively in one hand, taking no notice of his playful companions, but meditating, doubtless, upon the happiness he enjoyed in the unrestrained liberty of his native forests. It struck me that he might have a wife, and an interesting family of young monkeys, and was thinking of their unhappy fate, deprived of their natural protector. Who would now seek for them fruits and nuts, roots and juicy herbs?—who teach them to catch the bright-winged beetle—to rob the wild bee of its delicious honey—to rifle the bird's-nest—or to swing fear-

lessly by their tails from the topmost branches
of the loftiest trees? While engaged in these
painful reflections, I thought I perceived a tear
glistening in the creature's eye; and the better
to observe this evidence of his silent sorrow, I
drew close to the cage, and stooped down, when
the treacherous brute suddenly seized my new
Dunstable bonnet with a ferocious gripe, tore
the entire front of it away, and dragging it
through the bars into the cage, pulled it, before
my eyes, into fragments, which he distributed
amongst the other little wretches, who screamed
and chattered like so many demons in high glee
at my misfortune. I believe I must have looked
very ridiculous with the remains of my poor
bonnet, that cost me five and sixpence, exclusive
of the ribbons, which I got a bargain, being a
remnant purchased at Albert House, where, for
the last five years, they have been selling off the
remainder of their stock, in consequence of a
great fire, or a great flood, or an extensive bankruptcy, or an immediate pulling down of the
premises, which has compelled the proprietor to
make enormous sacrifices, every two or three
months, for the sole benefit of the public. I was
so dreadfully confused when I heard everybody
tittering and laughing around me, that I caught
Maria and Bella—who, poor things, being really
frightened had set up a violent screaming—and

hurrying away, prepared to return home as quickly as possible. Fortunately we found a cab outside the gate, into which we all got, and glad enough I was to escape from the impudent stares and scarcely suppressed laughter of every one we met, at my truly ridiculous *coiffure*,—as the French call anything that people stick on the head.

We got back to —— Square without any further accident, though my annoyances were not over; for during our ride home Frank, who had got hold of the check-string, kept pulling it and causing the driver to stop, that he might ask him some absurd question, such as, " Did he think the Bishop of Battersea was at home that morning?" or, " Would his horse like to stop and take forty winks?" until at length the man grew so angry, he paid no attention to the check-string when we really wanted him to pull up at our door; and I was obliged to put my head and the remains of my ruined Dunstable out of the window, and entreat him to stop, or Heaven knows where he might have carried us to.

# CHAPTER V.

DURING the two following days we were toler-
ably tranquil, and I really began to hope that
we should get through the holidays without any
serious disturbance. Frank had taken to the
study of Popular Chemistry, and had fitted up
a small room near the kitchen for a laboratory,
with shelves, and boxes, and crucibles, and fun-
nels, and syphons, and all manner of glasses and
crooked-necked bottles. He had a book which
contained directions for performing a number of
chemical experiments, " with perfect ease and
security by youth of both sexes;" but I really
think the author should be punished severely for
placing such a notorious falsehood on his title-
page; for if there ever was an invention by which
" ease " and " security " in a quiet family can be

destroyed, I do not hesitate to say it is Chemistry
at Home, as practised by young gentlemen of ingenious and mischievous tendencies. Mr. Pickleberry was rather pleased than otherwise at the
scientific fancy which had seized his son, having
an idea that if boys were left to pursue their own
tastes, they would naturally lead to something ;—
and so they did, in the case of Frank, who being
supplied with plenty of money to purchase che-
micals and apparatus, went to work vigorously,
and perfectly astonished Mary the cookmaid by
showing her a landscape, drawn with sympathetic
inks, representing a desolate winter scene, which,
on being held to the fire, assumed the appearance
of summer, with the fields and trees smiling in
their greenest livery. Theodore Tunks was admitted to the secrets of the laboratory, under a
solemn promise of strict silence respecting the
mysterious proceedings carried on there. He
was continually rushing out in a state of great
excitement and perspiration to the chemist's, for
papers and bottles of various articles required for
their experiments; and it was noticed by the servants that he began to talk wildly about alkalies
and acids, and oxides and gases, and about setting water on fire, and being able to make iron
that would not sink, and paper that would not
burn; and he quite alarmed the poor cook, who
was a credulous and timid person, by telling her

that she was composed principally of carbon, oxygen, hydrogen, and nitrogen. He also greatly scandalized the propriety of the kitchen, by maintaining that there was a simple affinity between Sarah the housemaid, and the serious butterman, who takes her regularly to the Reverend Mr. Bugsby's chapel, and now and then to the tee-total festivals of "The Young Men and Women's Cup-that-Cheers-but-not-Inebriates Association," where hot water and flatulent speeches are liberally supplied the company at sixpence per head. Nothing remarkable, however, took place for a couple of days beyond a frightful breakage of plates, and cups, and glasses, and an alarming alteration in the appearance of the page, who, from being entirely green, became speckled all over with rusty red blotches, that made him look like a spotted lizard—the effect, as I heard, of some acid having accidentally spattered over him while making an interesting experiment. Mr. and Mrs. Pickleberry had gone, I remember, to the opera in the evening; it was one of the nights that Grisi was to sing in a great part, and I was sitting alone in the nursery, fancying what an opera was like. Annette, who had been once in the gallery, with her aunt, on an order from one of the dressers of the theatre, who lodged in her house, tried to give me a description of it; but whether it was Annette's dul-

ness or mine, I can't say, but all I could understand was, that she thought they never would
have done mounting those stone stairs up to the
gallery, and when they got there it was so hot
and so crowded that they were nearly stifled—
the only seat they could obtain being on one of
the back benches, amongst some dirty-looking,
hairy-faced foreigners, who talked very loud in
an unintelligible language, and emitted a powerful flavour of garlic and tobacco.  She could not
say much about the music, which the chattering
of her neighbours prevented her hearing; nor
about the actors, whom she could not see; but
her aunt told her, when the audience laughed,
it was at Lablache, and when they cried " Brava !"
and " Encore !" it was for Grisi or Mario.  She,
however, enjoyed herself very much, as her aunt
had brought her pockets full of oranges and biscuits; and the foreign gentleman, who sat next
Annette, was exceedingly attentive, squeezing her
hand with an expression of tender ferocity in his
eyes, that was altogether irresistible.  Annette's
description of the opera did not, however, satisfy
me, and it was one of my favourite day-dreams
to picture to myself what it really was, or ought
to be, if I could have my wish.  I had fallen into
one of these reveries, and in imagination was
transported to the Opera-house, when suddenly I
heard something like a groan and a crash from

the lower part of the house, which in an instant
dispelled my vision, and caused me to fly downstairs.  When I think of it now, I am surprised
at my courage, for it might have been robbers
who had broken into the house, and had murdered the unfortunate cook, whom they found
alone in the kitchen.  I did not, however, give
myself time to reflect on the matter, but rushing
down in the dark, I stumbled over something
round and soft that lay in the passage near the
pantry.  A faint ray of light through the half-
open kitchen door, enabled me to perceive that
the bulk was an inanimate female body,—and, oh
Heavens ! how my blood grew cold, on examining
the features, to find that the victim was Mary,
the cookmaid !  I believe I fainted on the body
of the deceased, in the full conviction that I was
to be the next sacrifice—for I was unconscious of
what followed, until I became aware that Tunks
the speckled page was assiduously scorching my
nose with a feather-broom which he was burning
close under it.  Mary the cookmaid had recovered
from what was happily only a swoon, and was now
in a violent hysterical fit, kicking her heels with
energetic perseverance on the foot-mat in the passage ; while Annette and Master Frank, who looked
seriously alarmed, were dashing basins of cold
water in her face.  The cause of all this disturbance was, as usual, Master Frank :—but I am spared

the necessity of exposing his mischievous propen-
sities, as the whole affair is related in the following letter, written by Mary herself to her cousin
Polly Jenkins. How I got sight of it does not
matter, provided I can vouch for its authenticity,
which I certainly can.

"London, —— Squair;

"DEAR POLLY,              <i>Agosthefift,</i> 185—.

      "I set down in a state of grate pupplexity
and loness of spirts—conserning my futer prospex
and a heavy dinner—which I've just sent up.
Oh! Poll dear there's nothink but trubbles in
this sublimary world—the tubbot's biled to rags
—and the lobster sarse is spilte—and I've given
missus a month's warnin and told her to perwide
herself which I hope she may—and there's old
Stubbs—Missus's unkil from the sitty a-dining with
us who's as rich as Ajicu, and alwase blose up the
cook—if everythink aint right at dinner—won't he
be savidge about the tubbot!—that's one cumfurt
if it's the last I ever have in this ouse—wich is
an Ell upon Hearth sinse that imp of Mischif
Master Frank kem home for his Midsmmr holidays. But I must tell you ow it all appened. It was
last Wensday nite—Master and Missus had gone
to the hopra to ear Greasy—and Sarah tuck
the favrable hoppertunity of the Revrent Mr
Buggsby's heavening lectur with her young man

—and I was telling of my fortin aloan by the kitching fire—with a pack of cards wich I keep with my corjial mixtur in a Drawre of the dresser—for the releaf of my week mind. Well, if you'll beleave me Poll—as sure as you stand there I cut spades three times running wich is bad luck; then the King of Clubs, wich is Sam Stork the pellease-man—who as been paying me serous attentions for three months—turned up close to the quean of dimons—wich I suspex is the redhared cookmade at Number 19 that's been trying to induce Sam down her airey with all sorts of nice things—wich pelleasemen have a natural leaning to.—The thort of Sam's proving unconstant after so much pud-den quite overcum me, and if it hadn't bean for the corjial mixtur—and a good cry—I know I should have gone write hoff into a fit of asterisks. How-ever I kept up and began turning in my mind—what I could get for supper—inkase Sam come a coffin at the airey—wich he mostly does, aboutt ten oclok—when the fammalee is a broad. I recklected there was a nice wheel pie in the pantry wich I thort he'd like with a bit of briled bakun and a cupple of poarched hegs—and a small slice of pic-keld sammon or the leg of a rost goos and a plate of curn pie or sweet gelly to finish—for I know pore Sam's stummik is dellicatt. Cordingly I went to fetch the pie from the pantry in the dark —but oh Poll! when I hopend the dore what an

orrid fan-tom met my gays. There stood Sam
Stork in a suit of blew fire, bul's high and awl;—as
nateral as life;—and
to make it moar
effecting there was
rit under him in firy
letters the hawful
words ' MOVE ON!'
I felt my ed go
round the wheel pie
that I had ketch'd
hold on, and I fell
in a ded feint for
alfanour—and then
came two— though
I looked very one
all the next day.

MOVE ON !!!

But what do you think the fan-tom was, after all—
but a peace of Master Frank's fun.—He'd been and
drawed Sam Stork with Fossfuss on the wall wich
I never was so frikend in my life—though he tried
to make me beleave it was only a comical experi-
mence. Hows'ever I made up my mind to quit
the plaice—and next day I gev missus a month's
warnin—so Poll dear—I wish you'd look out for
a sootable sitivation for a planc cook ware the
waggis is good and they keep a full groan futman
wich they doan't hear—only a bit of a paige in a
grin jackit—wich is nothink in a kitching ware

there's a cook and an ousemade—beside the lady's made wich I doan't kount. So no moar at present dear Poll from your afflictuated cuzzin,

"MARY ROBINSON."

"PEA. S—I open my lettir to menshion I ave seen Sam Stork;—the cards were all rong Poll— he doan't care a might about that red-hared creetur at number 19,—for he toll'd me with his own lips—I was the bell of all the aireys—and sitch lips as he as Poll!—oh my!"

The affair with the cook and the phosphorus was the cause of Master Frank being "carpeted" —as he called it the next morning—by the "governor," who read him a severe lecture upon his mischievous pranks, and, I believe, threatened to send him to a school in Boulogne where the pupils were allowed no holidays, unless he behaved with greater propriety at home. The parental admonition was apparently not without effect; and for two or three days following, Frank's love of mischief only exhibited itself in the comparatively harmless amusement of tormenting Miss Crump, a crabbed old maid, who lived a few doors off, round the corner, by dazzling her, when the sun shone, with a looking-glass, from the parapet of our house, as she sat at work in her back parlour window. Poor Miss Crump—who had the misfortune of being short-sighted as well as short-tempered—took fire at the annoyance, but, being unable to discover the author of it, set it down in her mind that it could be no other than that dreadful one-eyed Captain Folkard, at Number 17, who wore those filthy moustaches, and was in the habit of smoking a large meerschaum in his garden in an old dressing-gown and military cap, and scandalizing the entire neighbourhood by singing, at the pitch of his stentorian voice, some awful song, of which every verse ended with—

"Whack, whack, whack!
Cigars and cognac!"

Moreover, the one-eyed Captain had a one-eyed terrier dog, called "Buffer," the ditto of its master and the terror of the feline race. It was reported he used to lie in ambush under a gooseberry-bush in the Captain's garden until an unsuspecting puss ventured across the wall, when the treacherous brute rushed out, and, seizing the hapless trespasser, generally finished its mortal career by a couple of vicious shakes. The Captain was strongly suspected of comforting and abetting "Buffer" in his cat-killing exploits; and the extraordinary bigness of the plums in his garden was accounted for by the number of murdered cats that had been secretly buried by him at the roots of a plum-tree to which he paid particular attention. Miss Crump was morally convinced that he was the inhuman destroyer of her beautiful tabby Tom, who had disappeared mysteriously one night; and she hated him accordingly with all the hate that an old maid might be supposed to feel under such aggravating circumstances. A bitter feud had consequently sprung up between Miss Crump and Captain Folkard, and several civil annoyances had been interchanged by them, especially when they met at the whist-parties in the neighbourhood, where Miss Crump's superior tact in discovering the enemy's weak points, and dexterously attacking them, provoked him to that degree that he frequently threw up his cards and left the table swelling with rage. Finding himself no match for Miss Crump in sarcasm, the Captain used to retaliate by practical jokes; so that she had no doubt it was he who was flashing the light across her eyes from his attic window. A messenger was therefore despatched by her to the Captain with the following note :—

"Miss CRUMP'S compliments to Captain FOLKARD—will thank him to refrain from reflecting upon her, as he has been doing all this day."

The Captain, who did not understand the meaning of the request, thought it a piece of polite impertinence, to which he replied, with military precision :—

"Captain FOLKARD'S compliments to Miss CRUMP. Whenever Captain F. reflects, it is not upon Miss CRUMP."

The lady felt that the Captain's sarcastic answer merited a rejoinder, and she wrote back :—

"Miss CRUMP is rejoiced to find that Captain FOLKARD can reflect upon anything."

The Captain, in a towering passion, responded thus :—

"Captain FOLKARD regrets to find that Miss CRUMP's head is, as usual, not quite right this evening."

With trembling hand the irate Miss Crump indited the following rejoinder :—

"Miss CRUMP requires from Captain FOLKARD an immediate explanation or an apology for his offensive assertion that her head is not quite right this evening."

Without delay, the Captain replied laconically :—

"Captain FOLKARD declines explanations. Captain F. never apologizes."

The lady now resumed her dignity, and informed Captain Folkard, in a formal note, that she meant to refer the matter to her lawyer, who, a couple of days after, served Captain Folkard with a notice of action for slander; having, in a letter to Miss Crump, alleged by implication that his client was in the habit of getting intoxicated in the evening, whereby her head had become affected.

The case, which excited a good deal of curiosity, was tried, after some delay, in the Queen's Bench,

I think, where a verdict was given for the plaintiff, with leave for the defendant to move for a new trial, which he did, and then the verdict being the other way, the lawyers on the opposite side raised some curious point of law by which they were able to have the whole business performed over again, before ever so many judges " sitting in error,"— which I'm afraid they often do. The affair, at all events, caused terrible discussions at the whist-parties, and was eventually the means of breaking up those pleasant little *soirées.*

This stupid squabble has already made me wander too far from my subject, so I shall not say another word about it, except that I was rather surprised, a few months ago, on reading the following announcement in the *Morning Post :—*

" MARRIED, on the —th of ——, Captain John Hardman Folkard, late of the Bengal Cavalry, to the lovely and accomplished Miss Virginia Helen Crump, both of —— Square. After the ceremony the happy couple left for the Lakes of Cumberland, amidst whose romantic scenery they intend passing the honeymoon. The marriage has, we understand, been the means of removing from the Courts of Law to the Court of Hymen the long-pending actions of 'Crump *versus* Folkard' and 'Folkard *versus* Crump,' which, it is to be hoped, will now be brought to an amicable termination."

# CHAPTER VI.

The Juvenile Party—Master Frank "At Home"—Arrival of
the Guests—Tea and Quadrilles—The Shy Boy and his Tormentors—Wonders of the Magic Lantern—An Old Picture
by a New Hand—Folkard at Waterloo.

WHILE the war which Frank had provoked was
raging between our angry neighbours, we enjoyed unusual tranquillity at our house; but as
the evening on which the important juvenile
party was to take place approached, there was
a deal of excitement and preparation amongst the
young folk.  First, there were invitations to be
written to all their friends and companions;
Frank undertaking to invite Jack Strangeways,
and Bob Smart, the three Bumpsteads, and Tom
Taggart, who I have already mentioned as being
remarkable for various accomplishments calcu-
lated to promote the hilarity of the party.  It was
settled that we were to have acted charades, and
round games, and forfeits, as well as quadrilles,
and blindman's buff, besides an exhibition of an
extraordinary character, which was not to be re-
vealed to any one until the eventful evening.

Mrs. Pickleberry having consented to become a martyr "for that night only," took care that the sacrifice she was about to make should be duly appreciated by those for whom it was made; for she repeatedly expressed her firm conviction that she should never survive *that* night, as she was unfortunately not blessed with the strong constitution of some women, who could endure forty or fifty children laughing, and shrieking, and talking all together. Neither her nerves or her head could stand it; but, of course, as a mother, she was bound to immolate herself for her little darlings, though Heaven knows if they ever would repay all she had suffered in mind and body for them. For her own part she believed all children were by nature selfish and ungrateful,—notwithstanding which, she was resolved to do her duty, by superintending the juvenile party, although she should expire in the performance of it. Mr. Pickleberry, who was generally engrossed either with his law-papers or his club, promised to "look in," if possible, on the "little people" some time in the course of the evening; and Captain Folkard, who was immensely popular at juvenile parties for his magic-lantern, his songs, recitations, and imitations of celebrated actors, had also consented to come to us on the important occasion.

Well, it came at last, and then came my trials.

Twenty times, at least, during the afternoon Mrs. Pickleberry's bell rang for me, and twenty times had I to listen to worrying complaints, commands and countermands, respecting the children's dress and appearance, or my own deportment before company in *her* house,—for I should mention that I was, on this occasion, permitted to appear in the drawing-room, but under restrictions so painful, that I would gladly have exchanged positions with Annette, who assisted Tunks that evening, and would have felt more independent and happier waiting upon the company, than making one in a society which I was plainly given to understand was entirely out of my sphere. Six times were the children reviewed by Mrs. Pickleberry before she was so far satisfied with their appearance as to say, in that resigned tone which she used when she had unfortunately nothing to find fault with, "There, take them away; I suppose you can't make them any better." I was then subjected to a severe inspection myself, and dismissed with a timely caution not to indulge in such boisterous spirits in the drawing-room, as I usually exhibited in the nursery. They should be boisterous spirits, indeed, not to be subdued by the icy sneer of Mrs. Pickleberry!

About seven o'clock—for it was to be an early party—the young guests began to arrive. Never, I believe, was there beheld, as on that night,

such a muster of pink sashes, and pink cheeks—
of laughing eyes and flaxen curls, dancing over
little plump fair necks—of merry girls and shy
boys, looking sheepishly conscious of having had
their heads recently operated upon by a fashionable hairdresser. " Rat-tat-a-rat-tat !" and " Tat-
a-rat-tatara-ra-tat !" went the hall-door knocker,
as it successively announced the arrival of the
fresh comers. Georgina, I must say, did the
honours of the reception very nicely ; and, under
the instructions of her mamma, showed that although only nine years old, she could appreciate
the higher claims on her attention possessed by
those young ladies who came in private broughams,
attended by a livery servant, over others who rode
in common cabs, with a number on the back.
Frank, I fear, allowed his natural feelings to get
the better of his respect for the usages of polite
society ; for he appeared far more delighted with
Jack Strangeways, and Bob Smart, and Tom Taggart—whom he welcomed with a cheery " Hallo !
old fellow !" from the top of the stairs—than with
the most distinguished of his aristocratic friends.
After tea, which was rather a formal proceeding,
and consisted chiefly in the consumption of macaroons and plum-cake, and the utter destruction
of two or three splendid frocks, by the accidental
overturning of cups of coffee, to the sore mortifica-
tion of the fair wearers, the room was cleared for

quadrilles. The two Misses Flathers, of Pembroke
Cottages, Kensington—sisters of Mrs. Pickleberry—having kindly consented to preside alternately at the piano, the young gentlemen proceeded, amidst a deal of pretty tittering and
blushing, and no slight degree of bashfulness on
both sides, to select their partners for the first
quadrille. Miss Hannah Flathers, who was not
on duty at the piano, acted as mistress of the
ceremonies; for poor Mrs. Pickleberry declared
herself utterly unequal to such Herculean exer-
tion. Frank danced the first set with Miss Ernestine Villiers, who was said to be a great heiress,
and was, moreover, a very pretty girl, with bright
blue eyes, and rose-bud lips. I was sorry, though,
he did not dance with Julia Mildmay—his "little
wife," as he used to call her before he went to
school, who, I believe, fancied he would have
asked her, and was so hurt by his neglect, that
she retired behind one of the window-curtains,
where she had a good cry to herself, and came
out, when the quadrille was over, with her eyes·
very red indeed. Frank, however, perceived the
fault he had committed, and endeavoured to re-
pair it by dancing all the remaining sets with
Julia, who soon forgot her annoyance, and was
the gayest and happiest of the throng for the rest
of the evening.

Little Egerton Paley, the shy orphan boy, to

whom Frank had been a sort of protector at school
—had entered the room unperceived; Tunks not
thinking it necessary to inconvenience himself by
announcing a person whom at a glance he pronounced to be " a snob." The poor boy, unable
to discover Frank amongst the company, felt so
much alarmed that he retreated to a corner of the
room, where, partly concealed by a gigantic china
jar, on a pedestal, he might have remained unnoticed all the night, had not Bob Smart discovered him; and with that peculiar instinct which
boys possess, perceived that he was a fit subject
to have " a game " with. At a signal from the
young wag, several of his friends came to his
assistance, and forming a semi-circle in front of
little Egerton, they commenced discussing, with
comic gravity, every peculiarity in his person and
apparel. His straight fair hair, his unfashionable
clothes, his Lisle-thread gloves, and unvarnished
shoes, were severally criticised as coolly as if the
poor boy, who sat trembling with shame and confusion before them, was a statue or a tailor's lay
figure. Some unusually clever joke produced an
explosion of laughter which attracted the attention of Frank, who, approaching the group, discovered instantly the nature and object of their
amusement. Breaking through the circle of
Egerton's juvenile tormentors, upon whom he
cast a glance that in another place might have

been accompanied by a more striking demonstration of his anger, he took the boy's hand in his, and shaking it warmly, told him how happy he was to see him. Cheered and assured by the kind and cordial manner of his friend, the timid boy gradually shook off his embarrassment; and when he was introduced by Frank to his sister Georgina as a partner in the next quadrille, he acquitted himself so well, that the eldest of the Misses Flathers, who had seen the Prince Regent dance, and therefore ought to know what dancing was, declared publicly that Master Paley was, next to Frank, the nicest dancer amongst all the young gentlemen in the room.

Immense was the sensation produced amongst the party by the arrival of Captain Folkard and his magic lantern, about nine o'clock. The mysterious instrument was carried behind the Captain in a square deal box, by Tunks, who placed it carefully on a table in the centre of the room, where it was viewed with intense interest, not unmixed with awe, by the juvenile assemblage, amongst whom a rumour had circulated that it contained a fearful collection of ghosts, goblins, and dancing skeletons—to say nothing of a curious illustration of the popular legend of "The Devil flying away with the little tailor, with the broad-cloth under his arm." While the Captain was unpacking his apparatus, Theodore Tunks was nailing a large

tablecloth against the wall, and the Misses Flathers and myself arranging the chairs and rout-
seats on the opposite side of the room, for the
accommodation of the spectators. All being
seated, and the candles put out, Miss Flathers
commenced the entertainment by playing a med-
ley overture on the piano, composed impromptu
for the occasion. Then Captain Folkard announced that he was going to open his comic
budget, with the celebrated " Plum-Pudding
Hunt ;" and after some shuffling and a few total
eclipses of the intensely bright disc thrown by
the lantern on the white cloth, there rose before
us an apparition of a magnificent plum-pudding,
furnished with a couple of spoons for legs, and a
knife and fork for arms. A crown of green leaves,
amidst which glowed the scarlet berries of the
holly, shadowed his brown features, upon which a
smile of hearty good humour seemed to play continually. A general cheer burst from the audience
on recognizing their old Christmas friend, who
suddenly started off, pursued by a lord mayor in
his robes, and close on his heels a beadle in his
cocked hat; then a tall Quaker; after him a
lawyer, and behind the lawyer a hen-pecked
husband carrying his termagant wife astride
on his shoulders; next a drunken cobbler; then a
wooden-legged Greenwich pensioner; a Welsh-
man mounted on a goat, and sweep on a donkey,

at whose tail half a dozen policemen were pulling. The merriment caused by the chase was immense, but no melodrama at the Adelphi theatre, with O. Smith in a favourite part, ever produced such a thrilling sensation as did the next "*tableau*," as the Captain called it, of a terrible ogre, named Hurlo Thrumbo, well known in fairy history, whose great goggle eyes rolled fearfully from side to side,—sitting opposite a huge pie, composed of little boys and girls, whom he transferred by twos and threes on an enormous fork to his gaping mouth. I felt Arabella and Maria crouching and clinging to me in trembling terror, and glad enough I was when Miss Flathers struck up a lively air, and the Captain commenced John Gilpin's ride to York, or Dick Turpin's ride to Ware, —I don't exactly remember which, but I know it was one or the other,—and very amusing it was. But I cannot describe all the droll things we saw; how we laughed at the two bulls tossing a corpulent alderman like a shuttlecock from one to another, and how we applauded the pretty picture of Cupid issuing out of the heart of a rose.

The great feature of the exhibition was, however, a panoramic illustration of the battle of Waterloo, with an explanatory lecture by the exhibitor, from which it would seem that it was the gallant Captain, and not the Duke of Wellington, who actually won that celebrated battle. It was something in this way:—" He, hem!—My dear young friends—the picture now before you represents the ever memorable and glorious battle of Waterloo—at which I had the honour to be present. Of course, ladies, you have heard of Waterloo — and Napoleon — and the Duke— that's the Duke there on horseback, on the right, under the lofty oak-tree, amongst whose branches the French shot rattled like hailstones in a storm. You perceive he's talking to a handsome young officer—hem! that's your humble servant — he — hem! I was thought rather a good-looking young fellow then by the ladies. The Duke is saying to me—' Fred, my boy!'—the Duke always called me Fred,—' these French *balls* are not so pleasant as the ambassador's *ball*, at Brussels, last night.' It is a remarkable fact, that this was the only pun the Duke was ever known to make, and this is the first time I ever mentioned it. You observe that cloud of smoke in the centre, proceeding from the French artillery, under cover of which three French columns, commanded by Marshal Ney, are advancing to attack Mont St. Jean. Our fellows received them in hollow squares, like masses of granite; but the fire was tremendous, and matters were beginning to look serious with us, by Jove! when we heard a distant cannonade. You should have seen the Duke's iron features relaxing into a grim smile, as he slapped his thigh, exclaiming—

" 'The Prussians, by —— !' I beg your pardon, ladies, the Duke did *not* swear.

" ' It may be Grouchy,' said Lord Hill.

" ' I'll bet a rump and dozen it's Bulow,' replied the Duke; ' I know the Prussian cannon. Fred, my boy, let's have a weed!'

" I handed the Duke a cigar from my case.

" 'I'd give half my dukedom,' said he, ' to have a despatch conveyed instantly to Bulow.'

" 'I'll do it, your grace,' said I; 'but I must have a fresh horse, for mine's done up."

" 'You shall have mine, my boy,' he replied, beckoning to an orderly in the rear, who held a beautiful Arabian charger, which he told me to mount, and, scribbling a few words with a pencil on a scrap of paper, placed it in my hands with this brief order :—

" 'For Bulow!' pointing his sword towards the Prussians, who had begun to show themselves on the crest of the hills. I understood all he would have said; and, laying my hand impressively on my heart, I exclaimed :—

" 'In fifteen minutes Bulow shall have it, if Folkard lives.'

" 'Pluck to the back-bone!' observed the Duke to Lord Hill.

" There are moments in our lives, ladies, when,

seized by an uncontrollable ardour, a man feels within himself that he is a hero. I clapped spurs to my charger, who, maddened by the thunder of the cannon, the roll of the drums, the braying of the trumpets, and the shrieks and shouts of the combatants, dashed down the steep like a whirl-wind, and, taking the bridle bit between his teeth, plunged across the muddy field right for the French lines; while, scarcely less excited than my horse, I gave him spur and rein, and in a few minutes, by Jove! we were within pistol-range of them. The enemy—struck, perhaps, with admira-tion at my temerity—opened their ranks, and honoured me, as I dashed through, with a hearty cheer instead of a volley, which I returned by the politest bow I could command under such extra-ordinary circumstances. In one minute and a half less than the time I had promised, the des-patch was in Bulow's hand. I need scarcely add, ladies, that it was to this unrecorded incident the victory was owing; for if Bulow had not received the despatch from the Duke he would never have made the manœuvre that gained the day. In fact, I may say, with becoming modesty, that Folkard won the battle of Waterloo, though Wel-lington got all the credit of it."

# CHAPTER VII.

A Scene of Confusion—"Music hath Charms"—Acted Charades
—Scene the First : A London Street—Open Air Performances
—Scene the Second : Dame Durden's Farm Yard—The Com-
batants—Scene the Third : The Beach at Brighton—A Family
Party afloat—Denouement, and Solution of the Charade.

THE Captain's narrative was received with
unanimous clapping of hands and stamping of
feet; and he was about to follow up the picture
of Waterloo with his terrific descent of the Falls
of Niagara, and a portrait of the Captain as he
appeared going over the Horse-shoe Fall in a
canoe, smoking his meerschaum and singing the
Canadian boat-glee, when we were disturbed by
a terrible fracas in the room. This, as I afterwards discovered, was caused by Master Taggart,
who, at Frank's instigation, had crept under the
table in the dark, and commenced his life-like
imitation of a cat and dog fighting.

"Gracious!" exclaimed Mrs. Pickleberry, in
accents of pitiable distress; "'tis my darling
Bijou! A strange cat has got into the room.

Will nobody light the candles? Miss Mims, where are you? what are you doing? Good heavens! if the cat should bite us! Miss Mims, take care of my darlings, will you; and my sweet Bijou?"

Captain Folkard, who, though a lion in the field, was a very mouse where a cat was in question, had seized his bamboo cane, and slashing desperately on all sides in the dark at the imaginary cat, succeeded in hitting the eldest Miss Flathers across the legs, who, jumping back, overturned one of the rout seats on which seven young ladies of tender years were seated side by side. I am utterly unable to describe the scene of confusion and terror that ensued. Most of the juvenile visitors set up a scream in chorus, until the candles were relighted by Annette and Theodore Tunks, who had been allowed to witness the exhibition outside the drawing-room door. Then a general search commenced for the malignant combatants; but not the slightest trace could be found of either. How they had disappeared nobody could imagine, except the perpetrators of the mischief, who, I noticed at the time, were laughing together in a corner. Mrs. Pickleberry, finding that her darling Bijou (who had been sleeping on his cushion in the dining-room) was still uninjured, and that there was no danger to be apprehended, swooned gently away, and was conveyed to bed with all the tenderness that a creature so fragile required.

This incident so disturbed the harmony of the evening, it was some time before it could be restored, although the Misses Flathers exerted themselves very much by vocalizing the celebrated duet from *Norma*, in the scene where the proud priestess commends her innocent children to the protection of her beautiful rival; to which Captain Folkard supplied a bass—quite of his own accord—and altogether independent of Bellini's music.

The Captain, who had a great genius for pantomime, next delighted the company by disguising himself as an old sailor who had lost one arm and one leg, and giving, in character, "The Bay of Biscay;" in which he was supposed, by those who had never heard old Braham, to excel that once popular singer.

After the Captain's exhibition, we cleared the room and had some Acted Charades, which produced a great deal of amusement, especially one invented by Frank, which was to be represented in three scenes of dumb show. Having selected his performers from the company, they retired to the green-room of the theatre, on the first-floor landing, where the actors studied their parts. The nursery was converted, for that night only, into a general dressing-room, while Annette,

Theodore Tunks, and myself, were requested to undertake the wardrobe and properties, for which an indiscriminating levy was made upon every box, trunk, press, drawer, and shelf in the house. Miss Flathers again presided at the piano, and played the overture to *Tancredi*, which had a very fine effect, when the folding-doors opened (for I should mention that the audience were seated in the back drawing-room), and the actors engaged in the scene were on the stage in the front drawing-room. The first portion of the word to be represented was " WEATHER," and to do this Jack Strangeways entered dressed as a street tumbler. The bodice of an old velvet gown of Mrs. Pickleberry's, ripped from the skirt and the sleeves taken out, served very well for the professional jacket; a pink slip of Georgina's was, by an ingenious adaptation, converted into something that resembled the garment which the Arabs wear as trowsers—the real trowsers being carefully tucked up and concealed underneath; while a fillet of blue ribbon tied round the performer's head completed his costume, which obtained three distinct rounds of applause from the audience. The showman's daughter, supposed to be an eminent ballet-dancer from the Opera, who sometimes condescended to amuse the public by performing a Highland-fling to select audiences in respectable private streets, was personated by Bob Smart, who had been accommodated with a plaid scarf and a nightgown, which he wore very short by way of a kilt. A cloth cap, squeezed into the Glengarry shape, with a turkey's wing-feather, from the poulterer's, stuck airily on one side, and stockings diagonally crossbarred with red and black chalk, gave him altogether a very theatrical and Scottish effect. The two performers were surrounded by a miscellaneous group of spectators, who had all come on the free list; there was the butcher's boy, with a real mutton-chop, kindly lent by the cook for the occasion, in a bread-tray on his shoulder; and the doctor's boy, with a basketful of phials for his master's dying patients; and the potboy, with half a dozen mugs, meant for pewterpots, slung over his shoulder; and a nurse, with a baby formed of a sofa-cushion, besides several other characters, who were all got up, as they say in the newspapers, with the utmost accuracy, and entirely regardless of expense. Then the showman, who had a bandbox for a drum suspended from his neck, and a set of Pandean pipes, composed of the keys of half a dozen trunks and presses, neatly tied between two bits of firewood and fastened under his chin, played a lively Scotch air, with the assistance of Tom Taggart, who was engaged to whistle the music behind the window-curtain; then the showman's daughter danced a Highland fling, in cha-

racter, with so much energy as to elicit a number
of white pasteboard shillings and sixpences from
a party of " fast " young gents who smoked
chocolate cigars on a sofa balcony, and a slight
sprinkling of brown-paper coppers from the admiring spectators in the street; then the showman was about to commence an extraordinary
performance *à la Risley*, with the sofa-cushion
child, which he had borrowed from the nurse-
maid, when a sudden shower of rain, produced
by Theodore Tunks pouring a quart of split
peas slowly into a clothes-basket outside the
drawing-room door, caused a general opening of
umbrellas and parasols. Some of the spectators
stood up for shelter under the mantel-piece,
and two stout gentlemen who had got no umbrellas made a simultaneous rush at the only cab
on the stand—an easy-chair Hansom—driven by
Bill Bumpstead, who had perched himself on the
music-stool behind. The two stout gentlemen,
having got into the cab on opposite sides, endeavoured each to eject the other, and in the
struggle fell backward into the muddy street;
a feat that appeared to be highly relished by
cabby, who, after the fashion of his vulgar race,
placed the end of his thumb to his nose, and
expanding his fingers winked alternately at the
prostrate pair. This being the end of the scene,
the folding-doors were closed and the audience

left · to discover the word that best described what they had witnessed.

" What can it be?" exclaimed Miss Flathers.

"Cab!" suggested the three Miss Parkers, in a breath.

"Dance!" cried an equal number of the Joneses, simultaneously.

" Jolly row!" observed Harry Bumpstead.

" Lark!" exclaimed Master Jones.

" Rain!" said Miss Hannah Flathers. "What do *you* think it is, Mrs. Parker?"

" Well, upon my word, I'm the worst person in the world to guess anything; but I should say it is something about those shocking show people that one sees performing in the street and a disagreeable difference between two gentlemen about a cab, or something of that sort."

"Could it be 'umbrella?'" said Master Fulton.

" Or ' parasol?'" interposed Ernestine Villiers.

" Depend upon it, it means something relating to the weather, and perhaps the word may be ' *weather*,'" said Miss Flathers.

" I'll write all our guesses down," said Miss Hannah Flathers, taking out her tablets and pencil; " and now be silent, for there's the bell for the overture to commence." And Miss Hannah having put down the several words suggested, went to the piano and again played the overture to *Tancredi* with increased vigour and brilliancy.

The key-word to the second scene was "Cock," which the actors proceeded to render intelligible in the following manner :—

The folding-doors opened, and a farm-yard was discovered. Little Alf's waggon and wheelbarrow, and the three wooden spades, which his sisters brought up from Margate-sands, were disposed so as to give an agricultural appearance to the scene ; but, in order that there might be no mistake about the matter, a large sheet of paper, upon which was legibly written—

### " DAME DURDEN'S FARM,"

wafered to a large folding screen, gave the audience to understand that the dame celebrated in song resided there. A cock crowing behind the sofa aroused the old woman, who entered from the farm-house, and pointing to the sun—a resplendent copper saucepan-lid, which had already risen above the horizon of the grand piano,—intimated, by holding up her fingers, that although it was five o'clock, her lazy servants were still snoring in bed. Snatching a stout broomstick, she expressed, by shaking it viciously, her intention of administering it indiscriminately to her household. She then returned into the house, while Miss Flathers, by previous arrangement, played on the piano the popular glee from *Guy Mannering,* which has something in it about—

" Uprouse ye, then, my merry, merry men."

Either the music or the broomstick of the angry dame, which could be heard distinctly thrashing the sofa-cushion behind the screen, produced the desired effect, for immediately there was a rush of male and female servants from the house. The men were appropriately dressed in wide-awake hats, with night-shirts for smock-frocks; some carried flails of walking-sticks, while others shouldered the wooden spades, and trudged slowly off to their daily labour. The maids—pretty creatures—carried each a joint of Frank's fishing-rod, with a twisted paper crook at the end, in the pure Arcadian style: they had the skirts of their frocks drawn tastefully through a pocket-hole at the side;—a fashion, I believe, generally followed by all shepherdesses who have good legs and short petticoats. They wore wreaths of artificial flowers too, and hats reversed for milking-pails on their heads. Tripping to the merry measure of a polka, the maids went off by the drawing-room door, for the purpose of tending the dame's flock on the attic stairs, and milking her cows, who were feeding in the rich pastures of the dining-parlour. The dame herself next entered, with a work-bag full of corn for her poultry. Opening the door of the poultry-house behind the sofa, Frank entered, in the character of a cock of the real Cochin-China breed, with tight, drab-coloured trousers, a zephyr paletot of the same hue, a feather-broom for a tail, and Mrs. Pickleberry's crimson velvet toque for a comb; he was attended by four interesting young hens, in polka jackets, to whom he paid the most absurd devotion, crowing and clapping his wings in a very arrogant manner, while the ladies were at breakfast. The dame having fed her fowls, returned to the house; when a shrill cock-crow on the landing caused the great foreigner to drop a splendid grain of corn, and to look rather alarmed. Then, a very small cock— represented by one of the little Bumpsteads—of the true English game breed, entered the farm-yard, and advancing boldly up to his Cochin-China rival, crowed defiantly in his face, and challenged him to single combat. The long-legged bully would willingly have made an inglorious retreat; but the presence of the ladies, and the impossibility of escaping, determined him to stand his ground. Whereupon, the rivals commenced a furious conflict, which was watched by the lady hens—who had finished their morning meal—with the utmost interest, and a secret hope that the gallant little English cock might prove victorious. The Chinese bird was by far stronger and larger than his antagonist; but the latter had spirit and activity, and by a dexterous blow of his long spurs—a couple of wooden skewers—he succeeded in disabling his enemy, who dropped on the floor in a swoon. The victor then standing upon his prostrate foe, crowed thrice triumphantly; whereupon Miss Flathers struck up *See the Conquering Hero Comes*, and the agitated hens advanced to offer their fluttering congratulations to the successful hero; while Dame Durden in the distance, armed with her terrible broomstick, appeared determined to avenge the defeat of her favourite bird. With this striking *tableau* the second scene finished, the folding-doors were again closed, and the excited company began eagerly guessing at the word they had seen represented. After many absurd attempts, Miss Hannah Flathers put down the words " fight," " farm," " dame," " cock," " rival," " victor," as being the most likely to help the solution of the charade.

The third scene—which, I should observe, gives the solution of the charade—was composed of the two words expressed in the preceding scenes. After the customary interval, which was filled up by Miss Hannah Flathers playing the overture to *Tancredi* for the third time, the action commenced. A placard hung against the wall informed the audience that they were to imagine themselves on " The Beach at Brighton." Then there entered an indulgent papa, carrying a roll of music for a telescope and wearing green spectacles, accompanied by an affectionate mamma with a basket, supposed to contain refreshments, and followed by six sweet pledges, who, by most expressive action, endeavoured to persuade the indulgent papa to take them for a sail in the open sofa-boat which lay on the beach, with a sweeping-brush mast and table-cloth sail. The indulgent parent shook his head, and intimated that the wind was not favourable by pointing to a curious effigy of a cock, constructed out of an old copy of *The Times*, and fastened to the end of Frank's fishing-rod, stuck up at the extremity of the chain pier of prostrate drawing-room chairs. The six pledges thereupon set up a simultaneous howl, and refused to be pacified even by the large oyster-shell biscuits which the affectionate mamma extracted from her basket and offered them, until the indulgent parent, turning his powerful telescope once more in the direction of the pier-head, perceived that the tail of the cock was then where its head had been a minute before. The wind had, in fact, changed, and was quite fair. The joyful fact being communicated to the pledges, was received by them with an exuberance of joy which manifested itself in an impromptu *pas d'ensemble;* while the indulgent parent poked an old tar (with a black stocking rolled up tight for a pigtail) who lay asleep on the sofa-cushion of his boat. The ancient mariner, glad to get a fare, immediately shoved his boat afloat, and, taking the whole party on board, loosed his tablecloth, and boldly seating himself in the stern of the sofa, called out to the lubbers to "splice the jigger, and keep the lee scuppers hard-a-port!" whereat the six pledges cheered vociferously; but the affectionate mamma, being somewhat alarmed at the sight of the green-baize waves, which were agitated violently by the two Bumpsteads, clung to the indulgent parent, who endeavoured to look calm and composed through his spectacles as the boat glided from the shore on its castors to the inspiriting music of *The Bay of Biscay.*

This being the concluding scene of the charade, the company set to guessing its meaning. Each guessed in turn, but none could hit on the word until it came to Egerton Paley, who instantly said "WEATHER-COCK!" This being declared the true solution, the shy little boy became a sort of lion for the remainder of the evening, greatly to the delight of Frank, who was too generous to feel the slightest degree of envy at the triumph of his young friend.

# CHAPTER VIII.

The Banquet—The Departure—Mrs. Pickleberry's Temper—
Visit to Astley's — Miss Flathers undertakes to pilot the
Party—The Hippodramatic Spectacle—Scenes in the Circle,
and Clown in the Ring—A Drunken Cabman—An Accident,
not unexpected—The Walk Home.

As it was now getting late, supper was announced, and the company descended to the
dining-room with more of eagerness than regu-
larity in their movements; but, by some accom-
modating process, they at length got seated comfortably, and grew amazingly merry upon the negus,
of which the larger components being sugar and
water, it was circulated freely amongst the guests.
I cannot attempt to describe all the choice viands
with which the tables were piled: the pyramids
of quartered oranges, the heaps of almonds and
raisins, the profusion of pears, apples, and grapes,
the abundance of jam and sweetmeats, the plates
of tarts, cheesecakes, macaroons, and biscuits,—
everything, in short, that could please the youth-
ful palate was there; and I feel bound to add,

that ample justice was done by the company to the banquet. But the brightest day must end; and pleasure too frequently proves as transient as the foam on a penny glass of sherbet. Twelve o'clock struck in the midst of a sharp fire of motto crackers, accompanied by shouts of laughter and cheers of uncontrolled delight. It was the signal for breaking up; and slowly and reluctantly did the young people, in obedience to the parental injunction, prepare to return with Jane, or James, or Mary, to their respective homes. The opportunity was, however, too favourable for trying a few practical jokes to be lost by Frank; and a good deal of confusion was caused by privately hiding away bonnets and shawls, and mixing caps, and cloaks, and strong shoes, and hats, and paletots, in a miscellaneous heap under the table in the back parlour. Julia Mildmay's victorine was discovered, after a tiresome search, stuffed into the pocket of Tom Taggart's paletot; and Fanny Parker's Berlin-wool hood, rolled up carefully in Jack Strangeway's comforter; and then, if Miss Villiers's warm gloves were not thrust into Tom Jones's galoshes! Altogether, I never was so worried in my life, getting things to rights; and all the while that impudent monkey Frank, and his friend Bob Smart, who is as bad as Frank, and I am sure was at the bottom of the mischief, stood snigger-

ing on the stairs, enjoying, no doubt, my per-
plexity. To add to my distress, that odious
Theodore Tunks had actually got intoxicated
upon half a bottle of sherry that he managed to
appropriate during the manufacture of the negus,
and was making a dreadful riot downstairs,
dancing the sailors' hornpipe upon the kitchen
table, and conducting himself in so very unbecoming a manner, that Mary the cook-maid, on
his attempting to kiss her, snatched him up, and,
being a stout girl, carried him bodily into the
wash-house, where, having first cooled his head
by a few plunges in a bucket of water, she left
him to recover himself at his leisure in a basket
of soiled linen.

At length the last of our visitors took their
departure—the last cab had rumbled from the
door, and right glad was I, when, having got all
my charge in their snug little nests, I crept to my
own bed, with my head throbbing so from fatigue
and excitement, that it was near daybreak before I fell asleep, and when I did, it was to dream
such a heap of rubbish, about being married to
a man made of fireworks, who exploded at the
altar, and went off in a shower of crackers and
golden rain.

It was late the following morning before I
could set the young ladies to their studies; the
dissipation of the preceding night had caused

them to sleep later than usual, and when I went into their room, at eight o'clock, and saw them looking like slumbering angels, so beautiful and innocent, I could not find it in my heart to wake them.

As I expected, the party furnished Mrs. Pickleberry with an unfailing subject for "knagging" at me in her own smooth, cutting way. It was wonderful how she used to connect every disagreeable occurrence in the family, with my "extraordinary conduct at the party." When little Alf caught the measles at the sea-side, six weeks after, she declared that "she had a presentiment of it ever since *that* night, when I would insist on making him eat so much almond-cake." I really believe it relieved the poor woman's mind to worry me, and that made me bear it patiently, for I thought, though it *was* hard to endure her ill-temper, that she suffered a deal more from it herself than I could possibly do.

Nothing particular occurred after the evening of the party until our visit to Astley's—a great event, which should not be unrecorded in these pages. The young people were almost wild with excitement, and I really believe I was almost as much a child as the youngest of them, although it was necessary to appear quite indifferent about the matter in the presence of the children, who were only too quick to perceive and presume upon

any little weakness I might exhibit. I had never
been to Astley's, and had only a very vague
notion of the entertainments from the large wood-
cuts I used to see on the blank walls and hoard-
ings about town, in which a horse was represented
performing actions that would require the united
qualifications of a cat, a bird, an elephant, and
a human being; besides, I was always making
mistakes, and confounding Mr. Widdicomb,* who
was admitted to be the hero of the ring at Astley's,
with Ben Caunt, who, I understood, was the cham-
pion of the ring somewhere else. Miss Flathers,
who had not been to an equestrian performance
since Ducrow brought out at this house the
*Battle of Waterloo*,—of which she always spoke
as of the actual event,—volunteered to accompany
us, and sleep that night at Mrs. Pickleberry's,
lest, as she said, the children might be alarmed
at the firing, which was really very terrific to
persons unaccustomed to it. Miss Flathers, I
should mention, believed that the celebrated battle
she had witnessed thirty years ago on these boards,

---

* Poor Widdicomb!—for so many years the "genius of the
ring," and the Adonis of the stage, at Astley's,—has made his
last bow, and retired from the world's scene. Immortalized by
the pen of Bon Gautier, and popularised by the wits of the day,
who ascribed to him a more than patriarchal age, with a per-
petual appearance of juvenility, Widdicomb became a celebrity
at Astley's, as Simpson, of polite memory, had been many years
ago at Vauxhall.

continued to be fought there every evening since, and was rather surprised when I showed her a play-bill, in which the piece to be performed that night was to be a "Grand mystical, romantic, demoniacal, legendary, and historical hippodramatic spectacle, entitled, *The Phantom Steed of the Bosphorus; or, the Demon of the Drachenfels,* with thrilling situations, startling effects, and novel illusions, never before attempted on any stage." Miss Flathers honoured us by taking an early dinner with us in the nursery, that there might be no delay; so we were all dressed and ready by four o'clock, although we were not to start till past six, which was certainly taking time by the forelock.

It struck me while we were waiting that I might blend a little instruction with amusement, by informing the children that the establishment we were about visiting was of such remote antiquity, that its origin was not mentioned by Pinnock or Goldsmith, in their valuable *Histories of England.* Frank here interposed to assure me I laboured under a slight error, for it was ascertained that an equestrian pavilion had been pitched on this spot by Hengist and Horsa, the Boneless Brothers of Bessarabia :—Hengist, however, unfortunately broke his neck while making his nine hundred and thirty-third successive back summersault, and Horsa became the sole proprietor

of the pavilion and the celebrated white horse of
Hanover, on which he astonished the Saxon public
by his daring equestrian performances.

What a wonderful bôy is Frank!

At a quarter-past six o'clock Tunks had a cab
at the door to convey us to the theatre. It was
no easy matter, though, to crush Miss Flathers—
who was what sailors call " broad in the beam "—
the three girls, and myself, into the vehicle, which
had been specially selected by Tunks for its large
size. Frank rode outside with the driver, and,
though I can't be positive on the point, I have a
strong suspicion that he smoked a cigar all the
way. Our ride was so pleasant, that we were at
the theatre before we thought we had got half the
distance, which so pleased Miss Flathers that she
engaged the cabman to call for us as soon as the
performances were over, and to insure his punc-
tuality she paid him his fare in advance, with the
strict injunction not to be too late.

"All right, ma'am! You just sing out 5944,
and I'll be there—safe!" said the cabman, hitch-
ing his loose great-coat on his shoulder, and
mounting his box.

Miss Flathers, who had undertaken the entire
guidance of our party, pushed boldly before us
through a pair of folding-doors covered with red
baize, above which the word "Boxes," in letters
of gold, caught the eye; and was advancing to

mount the stairs, when she was stopped by a gruff voice suddenly issuing from a little aperture in the wall, calling her to *" Pay here."*—Curious to see the proprietor of the voice, I peeped cautiously in through the hole, and beheld the head and shoulders of a stout, red-faced man, who had got a pile of silver and a pint of beer on the narrow shelf before him. I could not help thinking what a horrid life the poor man must lead ; for as there was no door that I could perceive to the den in which he was enclosed, and it would be utterly impossible a person of his bulk could get in and out through that aperture, I fancy he must have been put in when quite a baby, and that he had gradually enlarged there, like the great apples and strawberries I used to see when quite a little girl, growing inside narrow-necked bottles in country gardens. Poor man ! I wonder is he still living in that little den, or if he should happen to grow too big for it, what will become of him ?—Immediately on the demand for payment, Miss Flathers thrust her hand into her capacious pocket, and pulled out her purse, and, as Frank remarked, "forked out for the whole lot, like a brick." This done, we followed her in a flock up the broad stairs, and by the magic influence of a shilling slipped in the hand of the box-keeper, got comfortable places in a front row near the centre of the house. There was a pervading odour about the place, composed of various scents, the predominant being sawdust and orange peel, with a peculiar aroma of the stable, which I should say was more decided than agreeable. When people, however, come to Astley's, they must not fancy they are in the stalls of the Opera House. The band was playing away, with prodigious energy, a popular polka, in which the big drum and the trombone performed wonders, and entertained the audience till the rising of the curtain.

When I had a little recovered from the flurry of getting into our places, I began to look about to see what sort of a place it was, when a little bell tinkled, the orchestra left off making a noise, the curtain drew up, and the spectacle commenced with a view of the Blue Bosphorus, and the mystical rising of the demon steed from the waters, by the command of the Fiend of the Stalactite Caverns, who bestows him upon the Baron Shoutlowder, the wicked owner of the Castle of the Drachenfels. The baron accepts the gift upon the usual conditions, and leaping on his back, sets forth immediately on his journey to the palace of the Emperor of China, with whose lovely daughter, the Princess Narcissina, he is in love. While the magician is supposed to be performing this journey, a quarrel takes place between the low comedy man and the princess's maid, followed by a reconciliation, and concluded by a comic duet and a dance, which being always encored, gives the count time to have travelled several thousand miles, and transports the audience to the gardens of the Palace of Pekin, where the princess is discovered by Shoutlowder, sleeping in a bower of roses, who without disturbing her slumber, places her before him on the demon steed, and conveys her to his impregnable fortress of the Drachenfels. Raimondo, the young and interesting leader of a band of brigands, who secretly adores Narcissina, hearing of her abduction, calls his troop together, and relates to them his wonderful story, which produces such an effect upon them, that they take an unanimous oath on horseback to rescue the princess, and to annihilate Shoutlowder. The troop then gallop up a fearful precipice, which it seems is the shortest turnpike-road to the Drachenfels, where they arrive in the next scene, and bivouac by moonlight under the walls of the castle. Then comes a scene in Shoutlowder's baronial hall, where the baron and his vassals are discovered at a splendid banquet. Goblets of pure gold, filled with rosy wine, are quaffed by the company; and Shoutlowder drinking deeper than the others gets hilarious, and orders the " captive princess " to be brought before him. Obedient to his command, two of his minions conduct the princess to his presence, where he makes her an offer of his hand, which

she scornfully rejects, and gives him to understand that she will die rather than become "the
bride of a base tyrant," whereupon the tyrant
intimates that "force shall humble her proud
soul," and gives directions that she shall be "conveyed to the dungeon of the western tower;" a
decree that is about being executed, when a
trumpet is heard behind the scene, and a pale
supernumerary rushes on the stage to say, "The
foe is at the gate!" The princess, who knows it
is her brigand lover, drops on her knees to offer
up a prayer for his success; while Shoutlowder
rushes to assemble his vassals to resist the enemy.

The scene then changes to the walls of the
castle, where a terrible conflict is going forward.
Raimondo, at the head of his brave brigands,
attacks the fortress. A terrific explosion takes
place, which throws down the castle wall, and
discovers the Princess Narcissina in the tower
enveloped in flames and white muslin. Raimondo
hears her cries, and, clambering to her prison,
descends with his lovely burthen in his arms;
but the gallant youth is encountered by Shoutlowder on the demon steed, and a tremendous
combat takes place, in which Raimondo is over-
come by the supernatural power of his opponent,
who is about to seize the fainting princess, when
three distinct strokes are struck upon the gong.
The fiend of the Bosphorus rises through the

stage, and quietly beckons the baron, who, knowing that his time is up, relinquishes his prey, and,
uttering a horrid yell, descends with the demon
steed and the fiend through a trap-door to a place
I don't care to name. At the same moment the
scene opens at the back, and discloses a grand
*tableau* of the imperial court of Pekin, with the old
Emperor of China mounted on the Wise Elephant
of the East, and, surrounded by mandarins and
flying dragons, in the act of bestowing his
paternal benediction upon his daughter and the
brave brigand Raimondo amidst a dazzling display
of blue and red fire.

The spectacle which I have endeavoured to
describe was followed by " Scenes in the Circle,"
which, in my mind, were the best part of the
performances. What exclamations of delight and
admiration burst from the audience when a troop
of eight knights, in splendid armour and nodding
plumes, riding beside eight lovely ladies in magnificent habits, seemed to issue from the earth
into the arena! And how the children clapped
their little hands when the knights and their fair
partners took their places in the circle and danced
a double set of quadrilles! It was really wonderful how the horses set and *chasséed*, and went
in and out, and advanced and retired, and bowed
and curtseyed, and got through the figures without making a single mistake—which, as I ob-

served, was more than some of my young friends, who had the advantage of Mademoiselle Coupée's instructions, could probably do. Then there was the celebrated Abou Ben Hassan, the Child of the Desert, who, being a real Bedouin, rode as the Arabs do—standing on his head, with his horse at full speed. After the Bedouin came the Californian Courier, who performed a daring act of horsemanship; and the Wild Hunter of the Prairies, whose fearless riding on four bare-backed horses threw the spectators into ecstasies. And there was Mademoiselle Fleurette, who leaped over garters and through hoops; and La Petite Camille, a little creature, not taller than Maria, who danced a *pas seul* on horseback; and Mr. Dobson, the famous English character delineator, who appeared first as an old woman, then, in the twinkling of an eye, was transformed successively into a sailor, an Irish haymaker, a Scotch piper, and lastly, into a flying Mercury.

But all these, though very wonderful, did not produce so much amusement as the clown, whose jokes and conundrums, though of very ancient date, kept the house in peals of laughter. How they shouted when he saluted the audience with "How d'ye do to-morrow?" and how funny they thought him when he asked the riding-master if he should like to hear a good song; and being answered in the affirmative, said, "You had better then sing one yourself." And when he inquired why he was like the planet Saturn? and everybody "gave it up," he replied, "Because I'm the only *star* in this ring." And what sport it was to see him lift a straw off the ground as if it was a beam of timber, and stagger with it on his shoulder across the arena;—and how the children nearly went into fits when the riding-master rewarded some of his saucy jests with a cut of his whip round the legs, that made him jump like a skip-jack;—and what merriment it caused when Frank accidentally let his cap fall into the circus, and the clown picking it up, asked the audience, "Who dropped the pocket-handkerchief?"—and how the laughter was redoubled when the droll fellow, on discovering the owner, stuck it on the end of a pole, and with a profusion of bows and ceremonious politeness, thrust it up to Miss Flathers, who seemed rather confused by the general attention thus drawn upon her.

At length the performances terminated, and we rose to go away, conducted as on our entrance by Miss Flathers, who had undertaken the entire management of the party. On getting down to the entrance hall, we found it completely choked with people, whose outgoing seemed to have been stopped by some unexpected obstacle; men were buttoning their great-coats and turning the collars up to their ears, and women were drawing

cloaks and shawls tightly round their necks;
umbrellas were extracted from shiny black cases,
and white pocket-handkerchiefs tied carefully over
loves of bonnets, that had never seen two Sundays.
There could be no doubt about the fact; it was
raining, a perfect deluge. Miss Flathers, however,
felt no uneasiness about the matter, as she had
engaged a respectable, intelligent cabman, who
she knew was waiting for us; she had not forgotten his number—no, she was particular about
that;—and the horse she remarked was a grey
one.

Frank offered to look for the cab.

"No, my dear," said his aunt; "but you need
not get yourself wet; stand under the portico and
call, 'Number five thousand nine hundred and
forty-four.'"

"Number five thousand nine hundred and forty-
four!" shouted Frank.

"Five thousand nine hundred and forty-four!"
echoed the waterman with stentorian throat; but
though cab after cab came and went, none answered to "Five thousand nine hundred and forty-
four!"

"Frank has, perhaps, not given the right number!" said Miss Flathers, coming out to the portico, and raising her voice to its highest pitch,
called for "Cab!—Five thousand nine hundred
and forty-four!"

" Here you are, ma'am!" replied a foggy voice, as a cab rattled up to the portico.

" But you've not a grey horse, my good man, and that's not the cab I engaged—it was number five thousand nine hundred and forty-four!"

" All right, ma'am, this is forty-four!"

" Then what's become of the five thousand nine hundred?" inquired Miss Flathers.

" Just drew off with a party to John's Wood, ma'am!"

" John's Wood! after paying him five shillings to take us home! Mr. Policeman, what are we to do, if you please? It's really scandalous; I never was so cheated in my life! Five thousand nine hundred and forty-four is the number, and a grey horse!"

" Well, ma'am, I think you'd better have this cab; for there's no such number as five thousand nine hundred and forty-four, on any cab in London."

" Dear me; I suppose, then, it can't be helped. Here, Miss Mims; get in with the children. Frank, dear, you shan't ride outside in the rain; here, come in along with us,—it's only packing a little closer, if Miss Mims don't mind."

Of course, I said we could easily manage, by taking a couple of the young children on our knees;—though how we ever squeezed into that cab, I never could understand.

Away we went at a great rate across West-
minster Bridge.   Frank was delighted; but I
soon perceived, by the furious manner in which
the driver lashed his horse, and the sudden shocks
we received against the kerb-stones, in turning
the corners of the streets, that he was not sober.
I communicated my suspicions to Miss Flathers,
who, getting dreadfully alarmed, put her head out
of the window, and requested the man to drive
more slowly.

"You keep quiet, there," replied the cabman;
"I know what I'm about."

"But you'll upset us, my good man, if you
drive at this fearful rate," cried Miss Flathers.
"*Pray* don't go so fast."

The reply to this appeal was a renewed application of the whip to the poor horse, who was
now galloping furiously.

"Good heavens!" exclaimed Miss Flathers,
"we shall all be killed."

Frank tried to persuade us there was no danger;
but while he was speaking, the exhausted horse
slipped and fell; and the cab came, with a sudden
shock, to a stand-still.   Some persons passing by,
who witnessed the accident, opened the doors of
the cab, from which we made a precipitate escape.
The unfortunate animal lay motionless on the pave-
ment, while the drunken driver, who was tugging

viciously at one of the traces, muttered between his teeth—

"Here's a nice job!—shouldn't wonder if his leg was broke;—hold down his head, somebody—woah! I never druv an old 'ooman, that I hadn't some bad luck—waugh!" 

We did not stay to hear any more. Making our way out of the crowd, we collected our little folks, and, as the rain had pretty well ceased, and no cab was to be found, we determined to walk the remainder of the way home.

# CHAPTER IX.

Nocturnal Melody, inducing a Suspicion of a Secret Revel—
The Search—Love in a Bath, and Cupid in a Coal Vault—
Frank's genius takes a turn for Pyrotechnics, and develops
itself in home-made Firworks, which lead to a Blow-up,
and a Parochial Commotion—Imposing Appearance of the
Beadle on the Parish Engine—The Wrong Flue and the
Spoiled Dinner.

ARRIVING without the usual disturbance of a cab
at the door, I was about to knock, when Frank,
laying hold of my hand, and beckoning to his
aunt, asked us if we heard nothing. We listened
—and could clearly distinguish a full masculine
voice in the kitchen, singing the following lines
of a convivial song :—

> " Should any pain or care remain,
> Why, drown it in the bowl.
> Drown it in the bo-ho-ho-ho-owl—
> Drown it in the bo-ho-ho-ho————"

Miss Flathers instantly comprehended the whole
affair ; and resolving to act accordingly, gave a
loud knock at the door. The vocalist was struck
suddenly dumb in the midst of a prolonged shake

—the light, which we could see shining brightly between the chinks of the kitchen window-shutters, was instantly extinguished: and a clinking of plates and glasses, and a shuffling as of persons in confusion, reached our ears. After some delay, the door was opened by Sarah, the housemaid, who looked the picture of innocence, in a large night-cap and an old plaid shawl.

"Who have you got downstairs?" inquired Miss Flathers, who was aware that Mr. and Mrs. Pickleberry were out at a party, from which they were not expected home till four or five o'clock in the morning.

"Nobody but Mary, miss; who else do you think could be there?"

"I really don't know," replied Miss Flathers. "But if you have no objection, I'll see;" and taking the candle from Sarah's hand, she marched directly down to the kitchen, where she found Mary diligently employed smoothing the frill of a cap on an Italian-iron on the table.—I thought I perceived a flavour of gin punch as I entered the kitchen.—Miss Flathers sniffed two or three times suspiciously, but only said, "You are late at work, Mary."

"Yes, miss; doing up a few fine things," replied the cook, whose naturally florid complexion had faded to an ashy paleness.

Miss Flathers touched the Italian-iron as she

passed—*it was cold.* "I suspect you have some-body concealed here," said Miss Flathers.

"Goodness gracious, Miss Flathers! some-body here!—well, if I ever!—to suspect such a thing; but perhaps, miss, you'd like to search?"

"I should, certainly," said Miss Flathers, glancing under the table.

"Oh! very well, miss; please yourself. I'm sure I can have no objections. There's nobody here, miss,—nor here—nor here," said the cook, flinging open presses, and pulling out table drawers with an air of deeply-injured innocence. "I hope, miss, you're satisfied now!"

"It was very strange," Miss Flathers observed, as she completed her search of the kitchen, and looked into the bath-room. Some flannel bathing-dresses, sheets, and towels, had been thrown care-lessly into the empty bath, but the room was vacant. Frank, with something of a mischievous instinct, said nothing, but quietly turned the supply-cock of the bath; the water rushed in, and up started from beneath the sheets and towels Richard Gills, the butterman's serious assistant, who used to take Sarah to the Rev. Mr. Bugsby's chapel, trembling all over and with a countenance so dismal, that even Miss Flathers could not forbear a smile. Scarcely had we recovered from our surprise, than we were alarmed by Bijou who had come down stairs unperceived, and was barking violently in the coal-vault. The cause of the disturbance was, however, explained, when Sam Stork, the tall policeman, emerged from the vault, looking very black, and not particularly comfortable.

Oh, Mary! Oh, Sarah!

The two girls were in a pitiable state, and appeared so dreadfully ashamed of their conduct, that Frank, after the two lovers had sneaked away, interceded for them so warmly with his aunt, that she consented to keep the matter concealed from Mr. and Mrs. Pickleberry, on receiving a solemn promise from the culprits never to offend so again.

But I must now relate an occurrence of an alarming nature, which took place a few days after the juvenile party, and produced a good deal of commotion in the neighbourhood. Master Frank's thirst for chemical discovery was still as strong as ever; and having witnessed a grand display of fireworks at Vauxhall, his mind took a decided turn for Roman candles and sky-rockets, so he resolved, with the assistance of *The Pyrotechnist's Manual* and Theodore Tunks, to manufacture a few specimens for home consumption. I cannot tell the quantity of mealpowder, and sulphur, and charcoal, and saltpetre, and Heaven knows how many combustibles beside, that was smuggled by *that* page into the washhouse, where the operations were carried on with

the utmost secresy. I suspect, though, that Frank
had conciliated the cook, and that she was privately admitted to their confidence; for how else
should she have lent them a muslin sieve, and a
brass mortar to prepare their compounds, or how
did it happen they were drying their Catherine-
wheels and crackers over the kitchen-fire when
the accident I am going to relate took place, if
she had not known what they were about?—I
should like to know that. I had got through my
duties pretty comfortably that morning; the little
darlings had been washed and small-tooth-combed
without much grumbling—for though neither
washing or small-tooth-combing was in my agree-
ment, I always had to perform these operations,
as Annette's time was completely taken up with
Mrs. Pickleberry. I should not, however, have
much minded the additional labour, if Mrs. P.
had not been always wondering if I was not tired
of having nothing to do. I'm sure, if I was an
Industrious Flea or a little Busy Bee, I could not
have worked harder from morning till night. However, as I was saying, I had got through all my
duties of the morning, and had finished our lessons, including the multiplication-table,—which I
am free to own I never could quite conquer myself; but, of course, that is not of much consequence in a teacher, who has got the book in her
hand, and is only expected to communicate know-

ledge, not to possess it,—when I heard what seemed
to me a cannon-shot, and an awful rumbling in
the chimney. I started up and ran to the door,
dragging the children with me, expecting every
moment to see a shower of brickbats and chimney-
pots coming down the chimney, when Mrs. Pickleberry's bell rang so violently, that I rushed downstairs to see what had happened. On the landing I met that wretch Tunks, with a face as
black as an Ethiopian serenader's, who, in a few
words informed me that some of the fireworks had
ignited, and gone bang up the chimney, which
he was afraid was on fire. The latter part of his
story was confirmed by the sudden collection of
a crowd of people in the street, to whom the potboy at "The Spotted Dog" public-house, in the
next street, was describing something he had seen.
The parlour-windows were open, and I could distinctly hear, from behind the muslin curtains, the
conversation going forward outside.

"Here's a Bobby!" cried a shrill juvenile
voice in the outskirts of the crowd.

"Well, we ain't a-doin' nuffin', so we needn't
be afeard," said the potboy, who evidently understood his rights as a British subject.

"We're only follering our lawful calling. Fine
sparra-gra-a-a-ss!" added a perambulating coster-
monger.

"Well, what is it now?" inquired a stiff police-

man, stalking directly into the midst of the assemblage.

"Chimley a-fire, that's all!" replied a chorus
of bystanders.

"Where is it?"

"There!" replied twenty voices simultaneously,
while twenty hands pointed altogether, like the
witches in *Macbeth*, to our chimney.

"Who see it?"

"I see it," answered the potboy, authoritatively.

"What did you see?"

"I see somethin', just now, go fizzin' up into
the air, out of that big chimney-pot, with a shower
of sparks, and a lot o' smoke."

"There's more sparkses," shouted the shrill
voice on the flanks of the crowd.

Nobody doubted this additional fact, although
nobody had witnessed it.

"Send for the injines!" suggested several bystanders.

"Where's the turncock?" asked an indignant
parish-orator, whose withering denunciations of
the parochial authorities at vestry-meetings had
made churchwardens and overseers tremble in
their highlows. "Where's the turncock?—where's
the beadle?" reiterated the democratic Demos-
thenes; but before echo had time to answer the
important question, the turncock made his appearance, carrying on his shoulder a polished iron

BILL SMIFEL AND FRANK.      p. 121.

instrument, which I understood was the key of
the New River. In a few moments a splendid
jet of water, quite equal to those in Trafalgar
Square, was playing from a plug-hole in the middle
of the street, to the immense delight of the juvenile spectators, who cheered the turncock vociferously. More policemen now came upon the scene;
and presently the parish-engine, surmounted by
Chuffle, the beadle, who was also engine-keeper,
was dragged into the square, by a troop of idle
vagabonds. The apparition of the beadle, wearing his gold-laced hat, was the signal for renewed
cheering, which that beggar-dreaded functionary
did not deign to acknowledge; but descending
from his seat, knocked loudly at our door, which
was partly opened by Tunks.

"Got a chimney a-fire here, young feller?"
said Chuffle, squeezing his corpulent body into
the hall, followed closely by his lanky assistant,
Bill.

"Kitchen-chimney, I believe, sir!" replied
Tunks, respectfully.

"Let's see it, then."

Theodore preceded the parochial authorities to
the kitchen, where the beadle, having divested
himself of his official coat and hat, became a
common mortal, and set about investigating the
state of the chimney, which he declared to be
"afire wery bad indeed."

"We must get on the roof, Bill," observed Chuffle to his man, who replied by an assenting grunt.

"Got such a thing as a bucket o' coals in the house, young 'ooman? We must have a bucket o' coals to put out the fire," said the beadle.

"Certingly sir," replied Mary, who was standing with her hands clasped, and looking as pale as a sheet from excess of terror, running to the coal-cellar.

"Mind they're nubbly, cook," suggested Mr. Chuffle, calling after Mary, who speedily reappeared with a large bucket heaped with prime Wallsend.

"Now then, to the roof!" said Chuffle, leading the way; "and you follow with another bucket o' them coals young feller; they'll be all wanting."

We all proceeded in a body to the top of the house, where I expected to see the courageous Chuffle mount the ladder that conducted to the narrow trap-door in the roof; but, having measured the aperture with a mathematical eye, he said to his man :—

"Bill, I think you'd better go up yourself; and I'll hand you the coals."

Bill assented with another grunt, and, ascending the ladder, got through the trap-door without difficulty.

"Now Bill," said Chuffle, handing him up one of the buckets of coal; "you tumble 'em down the flue."

Bill intimated that he knew what he had to do without being taught; and vanished with the bucket. In a couple of minutes he again presented his grinning face at the trap-door.

"That's done, Mr. Chuffle; hand up another feed, please."

The second bucket was passed up to Bill, and we were congratulating ourselves on the assurance of the beadle, that the fire had been extinguished, when we were alarmed by a violent knocking at the street-door.

"Don't open the door," shouted Chuffle, from the head of the stairs; "I dare say 'tis another ingine; but we don't want 'em; we can do without 'em—we can. Pretty fellows, to come up when the fire's out, and expect to share our little fees. Don't let the wagabones in."

But the warning came too late. The door had been opened, and Mr. Smith, our next-door neighbour on the right, rushed in without his hat, looking very wild, and in a state of dreadful agitation. He had something in his hands rolled up in a cloth, which he uncovered with a ghastly smile that made my blood freeze, for at the first glance I perceived it was a blackened body, and imagination suggested it could only be

Mrs. Smith's baby, that had by some means
got burnt through our chimney taking fire.
Shutting my eyes, that the horrid object might
not again meet them, I sank, half-fainting, on a
chair in the hall.

"Here's a pretty business," said Smith, bitterly; "look, there's an object."

I would not have looked at it again for worlds.

"A beauty it was; so plump and large."

The pardonable partiality of a parent, I thought;
for I remembered the baby was a poor puny creature.

"The first of the season, too," added Smith,
deeply moved.

"What can he mean by the first baby of the
season?" I said to myself.

"A finer bird I never beheld——"

"A bird?" said I, opening my eyes.

"Yes, a bird; a lovely *young goose* that was
roasting for dinner, which has been destroyed by
a ton of coals being shot down the flue of my
kitchen chimney."

"Bill, you villain, you've made a nice job of
it," said Chuffle, in an undergrowl to his man.

The fact was, Bill had, by mistake, discharged
the buckets of coal into the wrong flue, at a
most inconvenient moment; for Mr. Smith's cook
had just placed to the fire a beautiful young
goose, which her master, who was somewhat of

an epicure, had purchased that morning in Leaden-hall Market, meaning to feast on it at dinner. Rumbling and rattling down the chimney came, in quick succession, the two charges of coal, accompanied by a mass of soot, and clouds of smoke, that enveloped in a suit of uniform black the goose, the cookmaid, and Mrs. Smith, who had put on a new silk gown, in which she was going to make some morning calls, when she unfortunately thought she would first step down to the kitchen and see if the cook was attending to the directions she had given about dinner.

I breathed more freely when I found it was not Mrs. Smith's dear baby that had been so dreadfully disfigured, and tried to appease the angry owner of the sooty goose, whose hopes of dinner had been cruelly blighted. As for Chuffle and his man Bill, they had the impudence to assert that, *if* the coals were thrown down Mr. Smith's chimney, it must have been afire too, and that, consikvently, Mr. Smith must pay for the services of the engine, the turncock, and the beadle, who had assisted in putting out the flames.

I really thought Smith would have knocked Chuffle down, so tremendous was his rage at this barefaced swindle. He, however, contented himself with threatening to make his grievance the subject of a letter in *The Times;* besides bringing

it before the parish at a vestry meeting, and
making Mr. Pickleberry responsible for the loss
of his goose, and the injury which Mrs. Smith's
silk gown had sustained.

# CHAPTER X.

Mysterious Disappearance of our Hero—Distress at Home—
Intelligence of the Fugitive, and a Visit to the Police Office
—A Disputed Claim to a Husband—The Lost One Found.

WHILE this scene was going forward, Mrs. Pickleberry had fallen into what she called a state
of "happy unconsciousness;" although it was
remarkable she could afterwards describe every
circumstance that had taken place during her
swoon—which lasted fully half an hour, in defi-
ance of sal volatile, burnt feathers, and hartshorn.
That she had not been killed on the spot by the
shock was, she averred, nothing less than a mira-
cle; indeed, she felt it had so shaken her vital
system, that her life now hung by the merest
fibre.

As for Master Frank, the cause of all these
mischances, he had disappeared no one could
tell where—on the first alarm of fire, and was
nowhere to be found, though we searched the
house from the attic to the cellar. When the
dinner-hour came, he was still absent; we were,

however, not very uneasy, as it was likely he had
gone to his aunts' at Kensington, to avoid the
punishment he richly deserved.   But when Theodore returned from Miss Flathers', where he had
been despatched for the truant, with the intelligence that he had not been there for three days,
I can't describe the state of alarm we were all
thrown into.   Mrs. Pickleberry called distractedly
for her "dear boy" and her "aromatic vinegar,"
and between the paroxysms of her maternal distress, upbraided me for not having taken better
care of her darling; and even went so far as to say
that I was secretly glad that he was gone, for she
perceived I never liked him, and, if the truth was
known, she should not wonder if I had instigated
him to run away,—it was just what she should
expect from me.

Mr. Pickleberry, a sensible, practical sort of
man, had the servants up to the drawing-room,
and held a sort of Court of Inquiry respecting
the origin of the fire, and the part that Frank
had taken it.   When he had finished, he put on
his hat without speaking (but I could see he
looked very pale and agitated) and went out,
leaving Mrs. Pickleberry in the care of Annette
and myself.   He did not return till near twelve
that night; and I could perceive by his grave
countenance he brought no good news.

"I have not been able, my dear Caroline, to

discover the least trace of the unhappy boy," said he, taking his wife's hand kindly in his; " but I have left a description of him at the police-offices, and have offered a reward for his discovery. The police are now on the alert, and with God's help, he will soon be restored to us."

" No," said Mrs. Pickleberry, obstinately re-solved to receive no comfort; "no; I shall never see my darling child again—never: he'll go to sea, and be eaten by the savages."

Mrs. Pickleberry had an idea, which nothing could disturb, that sailors and missionaries were the peculiar food upon which the natives of dis-tant regions principally subsisted; and she always connected, in her mind, a young minister or a midshipman with a cannibal pie, at the banquet of a chief in one of the South Sea islands.

" Let us leave his fate in the hands of a mer-ciful Providence, my love; and pray that HE way watch over and protect our boy, and give us fortitude to submit to His will, whatever it may be."

In this manner the father strove, by manly and religious exhortations, to console his poor weak wife; who, being as helpless in mind as she was in body, cried herself into a state of miserable composure, and went to bed.

For my own part, I did not get a wink of sleep all night, thinking what could have happened to the

K

poor truant, whose pranks I now heartily forgave, and would even willingly have endured them all over again to know that he was safe. As cab after cab rolled past during the night, my heart throbbed with expectation, or sunk with disappointment; fifty times I thought I heard his footsteps outside the hall door, and more than once I fancied I distinguished a timid ring at the area bell; but morning came, and no tidings of Frank. The children, who had heard that he was lost, spoke scarcely above their breath; even Georgina—whose tongue under ordinary circumstances chattered incessantly from morning to night—was silent, only venturing an occasional whisper, to ask me if I thought Frank had gone, like Robinson Crusoe, to live all alone on a desert island. We had just finished a melancholy breakfast, when Mr. Pickleberry came up to the nursery: it was the first time I had ever seen him there; and, really, if one of the giants of Guildhall had walked in, I could not have been more surprised; the children, too, were astonished at the unusual apparition of their papa in the nursery, and crowded around him with clamorous expressions of delight, which I vainly endeavoured to repress, while apologizing for the room being in such a " muddle."

" Never mind the poor things, Miss Mims; I dare say they are glad to see me," said he, smiling, and distributing kisses amongst the noisy candidates. "The room will do very well—I am not going to sit down:—I merely want you to put on your bonnet and come with me to Bow-street Police-office."

"Police-office, sir?" said I, trembling all over; "I hope—I hope, there is nothing——"

"Nothing that need alarm you," replied Mr. Pickleberry. "I have had tidings of Frank; the unfortunate boy has got himself into a terrible scrape, and I hear he is in a wretched plight; so you had better take some of his clothes with you."

There was no need to tell me to hasten; in less than five minutes I had put up a little bundle of Frank's things, and was tying on my bonnet in the hall, ready to accompany Mr. Pickleberry in the cab he had waiting to carry us to the police-office. As we rode along, he informed me, that a messenger from the station-house had brought him the painful intelligence, that his son was in custody upon a charge of having picked a lady's pocket on the preceding night.

"It's a wicked falsehood!" I exclaimed, and I felt the blood mounting to my cheeks with anger. "I'd like to see the wretch who dare accuse him of such a crime! He is as innocent of it as I am."

"I have no doubt of it," said Mr. Pickleberry;

"but innocence is not worth a straw if it cannot be made apparent to a police magistrate."

"But it shall—it must—it can't be otherwise!"

"I trust you may be right, Martha," said he, with evident anxiety; "but who can tell what imprudence Frank may not have been guilty of, to render him suspected?"

The cab had now reached the police-office, in front of which a crowd of curious idlers had assembled, in the expectation of getting a glimpse at a prisoner who was to be brought up on a charge of having four wives—all living—contrary to law. Three of the ladies, who had already arrived with parties of their respective friends, were engaged in an animated dispute in the outer room, touching the priority of their claims upon the accused, and the probability of any more wives "turning up" that morning. Stepping out of the cab I was astonished at the sensation my appearance produced among the bystanders, who pressed forward to stare at me, as I hurried up the steps to the door; and I could hear whispers of, "There—That's she—That's the fourth—They said she wouldn't appear agin him—She's not a bad sort, Jim—There's three more on 'em inside—Well, if he's married to more than two they can't touch him—Can't they though? you try it then, and marry three.—No! one's enough for me, Bill."

It was plain that the crowd outside mistook

me for one of the wives who had come to pro-
secute, and a similar idea having somehow got
possession of the minds of the three distressed
matrons, they rushed out of the waiting-room, and
overpowered me with interrogatories which I was
unable to answer.

"Well, mem," said the tallest of the three,
whose breath was redolent of gin and pepper-
mint; "you're another of the wretch's victims—
when was you married, mem?"

"Have you got your marriage-lines, *miss?*"
inquired a sharp-nosed, ferret-eyed little woman,
laying a peculiar stress on the last word. "I've got
mine here,"—exhibiting a dirty piece of crumpled
paper, which she held in her hand; "that's *my*
proof!"

"Ah, mem! your proof don't signify a straw,"
interrupted the third claimant, a short, fat, red-
faced matron; "I have witnesses to prove I was
married to him in Whitechapel Church, ten years
ago, which I was a plain cook at the time in Mile
End."

"We don't care what you was, mem; but you
must allow I was his first wife, and nothing
counts after."

"I beg your parding, mem; but I can't allow
no such a thing. Mr. Jabez Jones, my lawyer,
tells me, mem, that the pris'ner 'as got no wife
but me in the eye of the law, which I shall have

the pleasure of hanging him, or leastways of send-
ing him to the treadmill for eighteen months, for
the same."

"Do you mean to tell me, mem, that he's not
*my* husband?" screamed the little woman, thrusting the scrap of dirty paper under the nose of her
rival. "Is marriage-lines nothink, mem?—can
you show *your* marriage-lines?—I should think
not—I should *rayther* think not."

"It don't signify, mem," replied the other,
calmly. "I'm his lawful wife before the world;
and Mr. Jabez Jones, my lawyer, which is a
gentleman, living in Lyon's Inn, and he says
to me yesterday morning, 'Mrs. Smithwick,' says
he, 'you're a hinjered woman,' which I certingly
am, seeing I had five-and-twenty pound, and
a feather-bed and bolster, in the savings-bank,
when I married Tom Smithwick, which I was a
plain cook, ten years ago, in Whitechapel Church,
and, consequently, I'm Mrs. Smithwick—number
One; and Mr. Jabez Jones, my lawyer, says the
same."

"*You* Mrs. Smithwick—*you?*" shrieked the
weasen-faced wife. "Then, mem, who am I?"

The reply was prevented by the authoritative
voice of a policeman.

"Come, none o' this 'ere disturbance, ladies,
if you don't want to be locked up; clear the passage, will you?"

"But, sir, Mr. Jabez Jones, my lawyer, can tell you I'm a plain cook—leastways I was ten years ago—in Whitechapel Church, sir, and I challenge the world,—which I've got good witnesses, to deny it."

"Very well, you'd better tell that to the magistrate; but you really must clear the passage, ladies," said the policeman, thrusting the disputants and their friends indiscriminately into the waiting-room, to settle there their claims to the legal title of Mrs. Smithwick.

I was so confused by this scene, that I stood, not knowing which way to turn, for I had missed Mr. Pickleberry, when I saw him beckoning to me from the further end of the passage. I hurried to him, and followed him into a large whitewashed room, where I saw poor Frank, seated on a wooden bench that ran round the room. He was the picture of misery and penitence :—the dear boy's beautiful hair that used to curl naturally, hung in a tangled mat about his pale grimy face ; his cap was gone, and instead of his nice cloth paletot he had on a nasty, filthy fustian jacket, three times too big for him. His trousers, too, were torn and muddy, and the front of his shirt stained with blood. He looked dreadfully ashamed of his condition, and I don't mind confessing that I could not help bursting into tears, when he threw his arms about my neck, and, almost choked

by his sobs, protested he was guiltless of the
offence with which he was charged.   Mr. Pickleberry, who I saw was much moved though he
tried to maintain a severe composure, left the
room, and immediately after an old woman made
her appearance, with a basin and soap-and-water,
by the aid of which, and the change of clothes I
had brought, we soon made the poor boy look
something like himself.

# CHAPTER XI.

Frank's Story—Punch's Drama—A New Companion, and a
Visit to the "Royal Thespian Temple," terminating with a
Fight, which Frank wins, but loses his Clothes—Endeavours
to recover them, and gets into a Worse Scrape, which pro-
cures him an Introduction to Mr. Bodgers, the Magistrate—
Scene in a Police Court.

WHILE we were waiting for the case to be
called, I sat beside Frank, comforting him as well
as I could, and telling him he had nothing to fear,
as he had committed no crime.

"But," said I, "how ever did it happen you
were brought here on such a horrid charge? and
what has become of your clothes, that we found
you in the miserable rags you had on?"

"I'll tell you everything as it happened,
Martha; because you have been always kind to
me, and you don't believe I'm so bad a boy as
they'd make me out."

Then he commenced and related to me in his
own familiar schoolboy style all that had befallen
him from the time he left home.

" This was the way it was :—when there was
that dreadful alarm yesterday at our house,
through those Catherine-wheels and crackers,
which were drying in a stewpan over the kitchen-
fire, exploding and setting the chimney on fire,
I thought it better to run away to my aunts
Flathers—they're such trumps, you know—and
stop there till they got papa and mamma to forgive me.  So, as I was going, I saw Punch and
Judy round the corner—Punch is so funny,
Martha—and I thought I'd have a look at him.
There was a good crowd there, and the gentleman who played the Pandean pipes and the big
drum altogether—he was the manager, you know
—he said he was delighted to see such a respectable audience ; but though he was a gentleman of large property—and only did that sort
o' thing for the amusement of the British public
—he made it a rule never to perform in a private
street under a shilling ; however, as he happened
to be short of ' tin ' that morning, and hadn't
time to call on his friend the Governor of the
Bank of England for a couple of thousands, he
didn't mind, if they made up sixpence amongst
them, giving the whole performance as commanded by her Most Gracious Majesty and the
Lord Mayor of London at Windsor Castle.  Then
the dog Toby went round with the hat, and the
manager hoped we would act liberal, and encourage

native talent. There were a good many coppers dropped into the hat, and two or three unknown sums wrapped in paper came flying from the upper windows on both sides of the street; but the manager always found on counting the receipts that they were three halfpence short of the six-pence. After many vain appeals to the public, and several sudden appearances and disappearances of Punch himself, who was tootle-tooing behind the green-baize curtain in a very excited state, I made up the deficiency,—which had some-how increased to twopence halfpenny,—out of the three and fourpence I had left of my aunt Hannah's last half-sovereign 'tip.' Then I thought they were going to begin; but just as Punch had made his bow to the public, a policeman came up and ordered the establishment to ' move on.' Some of those who had paid their money grum-bled and wanted to have it back, you know; but the manager said, there was 'no money never returned;' but if the ladies and gentlemen chose, they might follow him into another street, where the police didn't object to the drama, and he'd be happy to give front places for nothing to all who had paid. I thought this was very fair; but a boy, who was standing beside me, gave it as his opinion, that it was 'all gammon,' and that the ' cove was a regular *do.*' Then he went on, and told me his name was Bill,—that he lived

' over there,' and he advised me not to waste any more of my money on such rubbish; but to come with him to the ' Royal Thespian Temple' —an out-and-out theatre somewhere near the Edgware-road, where they played the regular drama every half-hour. ' They're doing all this week,' says he, ' a stunning piece of intense domestic interest, called *The Strangled Sempstress and the Ferocious Footman; or, the Fatal Flat-iron and the Fiend of the Back Attic;* with lots of dancing by the Lothaire Family; and comic songs by Sim Crowle, the celebrated buffo vocalist of the Hall of Harmony. It's so jolly— and quite respectable too; tuppence boxes, and a penny pit.' I thought I'd like to see it, so you know we went to the boxes, and I paid for both. The theatre, which was down a dark passage, was a large room with a stage at the upper end, lighted by a chandelier made of a hoop stuck round with bits of candles. The place was very full when we came in, and very noisy; most of the audience were boys and girls, who were talking and laughing very loud while the performance was going on. Bill said it was ' chaff'——"

"What is chaff, Frank?" said I, interrupting him.

"Chaff? I believe it's a sort of cheap wit that low people, who can't afford better, throw at each other. Well, when it was all over—the drama, the comic singing, the dancing, and all—we came away; and there was a fight in the passage, and a big boy hit a little boy and knocked him down; so I said it was a shame, and when he wanted to strike the little fellow again while he was on the ground I wouldn't let him—and hit him. Then the other boys cried out, ' Bravo, young swell!' and Bill clapped me on the back, and said he'd stand by me if I had pluck to fight the other chap, so I said I would; and then there was a cheer, and the entire audience went with us to a court where the police never came, and there we had a fight; but first I took off my jacket and waistcoat, and gave them to Bill to hold for me. After I had licked the big boy I wanted to put on my clothes again; but Bill hadn't got them. He said he left them with another young gent, and nobody could tell what had become of him. Then I began to cry, for I was ashamed to go to my aunt's without my jacket or waistcoat; but Bill said he knew where to find 'the chap as had mizzled with them,' and if I'd come with him he'd get them back for me directly. So I gave eighteenpence—all the money I had —to a woman at a marine-store for an old fustian jacket, that Bill said fitted me as easy as a church! Then we went off together to look for the young gent, and we walked about the streets till I was so tired I could scarcely move.

"At last we got into Castle Market, where Bill said he had a little private business with a party he expected to meet; and bid me stop where I was, close to a butcher's stall; but presently he came running back in a great flurry, and whispered me as he passed—

"'Hook it! and meet me at the corner of Oxford Street.'

"But before I could ask him what he wanted me to hook, he was gone, and the butcher's boy had got hold of me by the collar."

This was his story, and a strange one it was; but I believed every word of it, and felt more than ever convinced that he had only been imprudent and incautious. I was going to ask him what grounds there were for suspecting that he had a hand in picking any one's pocket, when Mr. Pickleberry and a policeman came in to say that the case was about being called, and that we were to go into Court. Following the officer (who preceded us with "slow and martial stalk") into the justice-room, I crept into a corner, from whence, without being observed, I could witness the whole proceedings. Frank, I was delighted to see, was not placed at the bar, but was allowed to sit beside his father at the table below the bench. Mr. Bodgers, the sitting magistrate, who was intently engaged reading *The Times*, and giving prodigious decisions between the leading articles, did not notice the entrance of Frank and his father.

"Case of picking pockets, your worship," said the police serjeant. "Prosecutor is in attendance. Two prisoners, your worship."

"Very well; let them be put to the bar," said the worthy magistrate, without lifting his eyes from the paper.

"I mentioned to your worship — um - um - mmm—," said the magistrate's clerk, leaning towards the bench for the purpose of making a confidential communication to Mr. Bodgers, which I could not hear.

"Oh—ah—yes; I see—I see," said the magistrate, examining the charge-sheet; "quite right; William Smiffel and Francis Pickleberry. Humph! I know." Then looking round the Court through his folding glasses until he discovered Mr. Pickleberry, with whom he was slightly acquainted, he bowed to him, and, having scrutinized Frank with the eye of a man well acquainted with villainy in every form, he folded up *The Times,* and went regularly to business. I felt myself shake like a jelly when the magistrate inquired, in a very awful voice—

"Where's the prosecutor?"

"Now then, ma'am, get into the box, please; and don't keep the Court a waiting for you all day," remonstrated the policeman, who was endeavouring, with all his strength, to crush a corpulent woman into the witness-box.

"There are two persons charged here with having picked the pocket of Mrs. Martha Gribbins——"

"A green purse, if you please sir, with steel-bead tassels——"

"Si-ilence!" growled the usher of the Court.

"Where's the prisoner Smiffel?" said the magistrate.

"Bill Smiffel, come for'ard," cried the usher.

"What d'ye want on me now?" replied a shrill voice issuing from the bar, above which a pair of small glittering eyes might be seen peering watchfully in every direction round the Court.

"Put him up, that we may see him," said Mr. Bodgers.

The little creature was placed by a policeman standing upon a chair, and, being now more exposed to view, exhibited a countenance in which, although the features were those of a child, no trace of childish character remained. Hunger and poverty had written in rigid lines their experience on his pale cheek; and vice had set her indelible mark upon his shameless brow.

"That's one of them!" cried Mrs. Gribbins.

"You mustn't speak, ma'am," said the policeman who stood beside the witness.

" It was a green purse, your worship, with steel-bead tassels——"

" Si-ilence !" roared the usher, frowning awfully at the witness.

" So I find you here again !" said the magistrate, who recognized the prisoner as an incorrigible offender.

" Yes, guv'ner; but 'pon my word and honor, sir, I aint done nuffin this time; if you'll believe me, sir, I'm as hinnocent as a babe wot's un-borned, I am,—that's the blessed truth,—'pon my word and honor it is, sir. I don't tell you no lie, sir, cos it aint no use deceivin' on you, sir;—I arns my livin' honestly, and has guv up them games as gits a fellow into trouble."

" I'm glad of it," said Mr. Bodgers drily; " but what do you say to the charge of picking this lady's pocket ?"

" A green purse, your worship, with——"

" You must keep quiet," growled the policeman, pulling Mrs. Gribbins back.

" I never see it, your worship;—it warn't found with me;—there's no evidence agin me. It's werry hard a hinnocent chap like me should be pulled up, when I aint done nuffin," replied the young prisoner, drawing the back of his dirty little hand across his eyes, to make believe he was wiping away the tears.

L

"Will you relate, ma'am, how you lost your purse?" said the magistrate, addressing the prosecutor.

"Cert'nly, sir,—your worship. Gribbins is my name—Martha Gribbins, if you please sir. Twenty-two years I've been married next Michaelmas, and I never was in a P'leese Court in my life,—never was, I assure you, sir;—and it was only this morning I was saying to Mrs. Watson——"

"Never mind Mrs. Watson, ma'am, but tell us how you lost your purse," interrupted the magistrate.

"Cert'nly, sir,—your worship. It was in Covent Garden—not in Covent Garden, but in St. Martin's-lane, where I'd been calling on a friend in the Borough—Mrs. Watson her name is—she's in the millinery and cigar line, and a very respectable woman she is——"

"Pray, madam, keep to the facts. What were you doing in St. Martin's-lane ?"

"Doing !—I was coming from Covent Garden, sir,—your worship, where I'd bought a pottle of lovely strawberries. I'm very fond of strawberries in the season; only they are such horrid impostors, filling the pottle full of leaves, and sticking half a dozen strawberries on the top; but there's roguery in all trades, as Mrs. Watson said to me this very morning."

"Have the goodness, madam, to tell your story

briefly; the time of the Court must not be wasted."

" Cert'nly not, sir,—your worship. It was in Tottenham-court-road——"

" You said just now it was in St. Martin's-lane."

" Well, it *was* in St. Martin's-lane, I was turning over in my mind what Mrs. Watson said to me this very morning——"

" We don't want to hear what Mrs. Watson said to you; let us get on to Tottenham-court-road as fast as you can, my good woman. What occurred to you in Tottenham-court-road?"

" Well, it wasn't exactly in Tottenham-court-road; for I remembered when I got there I had to go round by Oxford-street to Castle-market, to buy a bit of pork for my Sunday's dinner——"

" To the point," cried Mr. Bodgers, angrily.

" Cert'nly, sir, — your worship. It was as lovely a loin of dairy-fed pork as your worship ever looked upon; my husband fancies the loin, so I thought I'd give him a little treat;—two-and-twenty years we've been man and wife, sir, and I can honestly say he never lifted his hand to me in anger,—unless when he had a drop in,—which isn't often,—not more than twice or three times a week, sir, and then he certainly does use me shocking, as Mrs. Watson knows;—she's a lady in the millinery and cigar line, sir, and lives in the Borough——"

" I must dismiss this charge, Mrs. Gribbins, if you persist in talking in this discursive manner. You were in Castle-market, you say, purchasing a piece of pork :—what happened there?" said Mr. Bodgers, endeavouring to bring back the witness to the point from whence she had strayed.

" Four pounds and a half, sir,—your worship, at sevenpence farthing a pound, come to——"

" Come to the point, ma'am," cried the magistrate, knocking the desk impatiently with his knuckles.

" Two and elevenpence, sir,—your worship,—three shillings all but a penny; so I put my hand in my pocket for my purse,—a green purse, your worship, with steel bead tassels——"

" Pray, Mrs. Gribbins——"

" That's right, sir; Gribbins is my name—Martha Gribbins, your worship. I'm not ashamed of it, nowhere, for I've been married two-and-twenty years, as Mrs. Watson knows——"

" Never mind Mrs. Watson, but tell us about your purse. You put your hand in your pocket, and found your purse was gone, I suppose?" suggested the magistrate.

" Cert'nly it was, sir, — your worship; and when I turned sharp round I saw that boy standing close beside me," pointing to Bill Smiffel, whose countenance at the moment exhibited a well-feigned expression of astonishment.

" Did ever anybody hear the like o' that? How could I have took the pus, when I never see it? You didn't see me take it, ma-arm?"

" Cert'nly not," replied the prosecutrix; "but you run away when I called 'Stop thief!'"

" Well, ma'am, there ain't no harm in running, is there? When I heard you holler out 'Stop thief!' I nat'rally ran, because I knew the p'lice had a spite agin me, and I thought it better to keep out o' their way, which you'd ha' done the same yourself, wouldn't you?"

The boy at the butcher's shop being next called, deposed that he had observed Bill Smiffel and Frank loitering near the spot while Mrs. Gribbins was bargaining for the pork, and when that lady cried out that her purse was gone, he ran out of the shop and laid hold of Frank, upon whom, on being searched, the purse was found.

Mr. Bodgers looked uncommonly grave, and I saw Frank turn as pale as a sheet, and glance anxiously towards his father; as for myself I felt as if I should sink through the floor, for I thought nothing could save him.

I had given up all for lost, and was wondering why Mr. Pickleberry did not offer to speak for the poor boy, when another witness was called—a Detective, I think they said he was—and he soon gave another colour to the business. It seems he had been watching the movements of Bill Smiffel for some time, and saw him pick Mrs. Gribbins' pocket; but before he could get away with his plunder, the woman had discovered her loss, and turning quickly round, the young thief, unperceived by Frank, dexterously slipped the purse into the gaping pocket of the fustian-jacket which the latter wore, and darted like a Scotch terrier under a market-cart, only to fall into the clutches of the Detective, who lay in ambush on the other side.

" There is no evidence," said the " worthy magistrate," as Mr. Bodgers was invariably styled in the police reports, " there is no evidence whatever to implicate this young gentleman," waving his glasses benignly towards Frank, " in the fact of picking Mrs. Gribbins' pocket; nor has it been shown that he was knowingly a receiver of the stolen property placed in his possession by the prisoner at the bar, who, though young, has the reputation of being one of the most dexterous pickpockets in London."

" Thank yer worship!" cried Master Smiffel, apparently gratified by the compliment paid him by the bench.

" It seems strange, however, that a respectable lad should be found in the company of a notorious thief, in the public streets. This requires to be explained," said Mr. Bodgers.

Frank held down his head, and made no attempt to reply.

"Let him answer for himself," said Mr. Pickleberry; "I know, at least, that he will tell the truth."

"I *will* tell the truth," said the noble boy, suddenly brightening up, and with his head erect, and his clear blue eye looking directly in the magistrate's face, he repeated the story he had already told me; with this difference, that he now spoke with a modest ingenuous earnestness, unlike his usual schoolboy style, which I could perceive produced its effect on the mind of the magistrate, who, when he had finished, congratulated him upon having escaped so well from the gang of juvenile delinquents, into whose company he had unguardedly fallen. Mr. Bodgers then told Frank he was discharged, without the slightest imputation on his character; and concluded by recommending Master Bill Smiffel to a three months' retreat at Cold Bath Fields, an intimation that seemed to afford little gratification to the young conveyancer, who quitted the bar, protesting that all the "beaks" and "bobbies" in London were his enemies, and meant to ruin his prospects in life.

# CHAPTER XII.

The Truant sentenced to Solitary Confinement—Musings in the "Museum" (*not* the British)—Frank writes his own Epitaph, and resolves to quit this Miserable World—Dropping a Line to a Friend—Roast Lamb and Weak Human Nature—Angling in Prison—The Poultry Show—The Release.

MR. PICKLEBERRY was naturally rejoiced at the result of the proceedings, and I really believe he was not so very angry with Frank; but he felt it his duty to exhibit some displeasure on the occasion, in order to make an impression on the mind of the volatile boy, whose heedlessness and love of practical fun were continually getting him into scrapes. Accordingly, when we got home, Frank was ordered by his father into solitary confinement in a sort of waste-room that we called " the Museum," because it was used only for keeping odds and ends of out-of-the-way things that nobody ever wanted or cared for or thought about, although many of them had in their day performed important parts in the world. There were large boxes of family papers and old letters, in which the confided joys and sorrows, the hopes and fears, the passions and the projects, that filled many a throbbing heart, now lay like those hearts mouldering in dark forgetfulness. There were shelves too—piled with musty books, that, like decayed beauties, had long outlived their time— almanacs whose dates reminded us of important events recorded in *Goldsmith's History of England*—sharp political pamphlets that had lost their pungency by time—stupid Acts of Parliament repealed by others still more stupid—treatises on legal, medical, and scientific subjects, swamped long ago in the tide of advancing knowledge and civilization. There were tracts with such titles as —*Hints on the State of Publick Affairs*—*Schemes for Peopling our American Colonies*—*Plans for paying off the National Debt*—*Suggestions for increasing the Revenue*—*Plain advice to the W—g Adm-n-tra-n* —*Strictures on the Hair-powder Tax*—*Groans from the Buckle-makers of Great Britain*—*Reflections on the late War*, and *Thoughts upon the threatened Invasion*, with other works equally attractive to readers of the present day. There were, besides, objects in "the Museum" which had been preserved from the dust-hole, the rag-basket, or the broker's shop, by associations that gave them a kind of drowsy interest in the minds of their possessors. On one side of the room a pair of mouldy top-boots stood stiffly on their former respectability; and suspended on a couple of pegs above

them was a coat, said to have once been scarlet;
with a pair of shrivelled leather not-to-be-hinted-
ats, worn by Mr. Pickleberry in his " salad days "
when he was at Oxford, and hunted with the
Neck-or-Nothing hounds. Over the fireplace hung
a driving-whip, with a silver-handle, which had
been presented him by the Four-in-Hand Club;
and flung in a corner an old battered lantern
and a bunch of street-door knockers, of whose
history I could discover nothing, though they
were probably in some way connected with Mr.
P.'s early legal pursuits, when he was a student in
the Inner Temple. A fishing-rod and a landing-
net remained as memorials of his piscatorial exploits, and an old-fashioned easy-chair preserved
green the memory of Mrs. Bramwig, the mother
of Mrs. Pickleberry, a famous whist-player in her
time, who died in that chair at the card-table,
in her eighty-fourth year, with these memorable
words on her lips—" Two by honours, and the
odd trick." A cavalry sword and a black silk
petticoat hung lovingly side by side near a barrister's wig and a brass dog-collar; a terrestrial
globe, from which nearly half the continent of
Europe had been obliterated, was concealed by
a broken Indian fire-screen; and a noseless bust of
William Pitt was huddled amongst half a dozen
flower-pots, in which the brown skeletons of as
many decayed geraniums remained the mementos

of long-departed verdure. These, and other odd pieces of unthought-of lumber, with a couple of broken chairs of different patterns, and an old deal table, were the principal "features," I think they call them, of the "Museum" in which Frank was now confined a state prisoner.

People have a natural sympathy with prisoners, and a desire to know all the minute incidents and employments by which the tedious hours in a captive's solitary life are filled up. It is some feeling of this kind, I suppose, that makes the adventures of Robinson Crusoe, and the memoirs of Baron Trenck, Latude, Silvio Pellico, and other remarkable prisoners, more interesting to the generality of readers than any work of fiction.

Some time after the events I am now relating, I found behind the window-shutter of Frank's bedroom an old copybook, in which he had scribbled some memoranda, in the form of a journal, during his imprisonment; supplying all the information necessary to satisfy the curiosity of those who may seek to penetrate the "secrets of his prison-house."—Here they are, transcribed, without note or emendation, from the original, as I found it :—

"THE MUSEUM.

"*Half-past* 12 *o'clock.*

"Here I am, locked up in this old musty lumber-room, 'during pleasure,' as papa says, though I can't

see where the pleasure can be. I suppose I shall be
kept here for the remainder of my miserable days.
Hush!—there's a mouse scratching in that corner
—perhaps 'tis a rat! I wish I had ' Vixen' here,
she's such a good one for rats. I dare say I shall
be dead before night—I know I shall. The door
is double-locked, and I have no companions but a
pewter syringe, and my Virgil. I hope when
I'm no more they'll give it to Jack Strangeways
—the syringe, I mean, not the Virgil, which I
know he hates; he'll find it convenient for playing
on the neighbouring inhabitants when he's home
for the holidays. It's a mouse!—I saw the fellow
peeping from behind a bundle of old papers in the
corner. Oh, dear!—I feel so wretched!        *
            *        *        *        *        *

        *        *        I've been looking out of my
window, but can see nothing but the waterbutt
in Smith's yard, on one side, and the poultry in
Bagster's on the other. I wish old Virgil was
burnt—I've got a hundred lines of him to trans-
late by six o'clock;—but I shall be dead and done
with Virgil and all my troubles before then.——
I wonder, will Julia Mildmay ever think of me
when I'm gone—Julia is a nice girl, and I think
I like her better than Ernestine Villiers, who,
I'm afraid, is a bit of a flirt, for I saw Tom Taggart, when we played at forfeits, kiss her twice,
though he ought only have kissed her once—and

*she didn't tell.* I'll write to Julia Mildmay, and tell her I loved her to the last.  *  *

\*     \*     \*     \*     \*

" I can't get further than 'Dear Julia!'—Never mind — I don't care how soon I'm out of this miserable world ; only I should like first to try my new peashooter at Monsieur Deville the French master's green spectacles.—There's a cock with a bad cold crowing in Bagster's yard ;—it's the old cinnamon-coloured Cochin-China fellow—I know his croaky voice.

" Now I begin to think of my faults.—I hope my friends will pay my debts;—they're rather heavy this last half; let me see—there's two-and-six to Tom Newsome—and three-and-four-pence to the apple-woman—and one-and-sixpence to Sam Spearing for doing my imposition—oh dear !—I'm afraid I've been very extravagant—but it don't matter when one's dead—does it ?

"There's the church clock struck one, and I haven't done a line of my translation yet—Hark !—there's the mouse again—ah ! he's off—Look out, old fellow, the next time you show your nose——What a beautiful day it is !—wouldn't it be jolly to be out bird-nesting — or fishing — or eating pork pies and drinking ginger-beer under a tree in Greenwich Park ?—But there's that bothering Virgil—let's see what I've got to do—

" ' Æneas celsa in puppi '—(Æneas was a tall

puppy). 'Jam certus eundi'—(I'm certain of this). 'Carpebat somnos'—(I should like forty winks). 'Rebus jam ritè paratis'—(also some jam properly prepared).

"That's what I call a free-and-easy translation. Oh, my! I'm getting awfully fagged—Hollo! there's the mouse again—so-oh!—I'll shy old Virgil at him—bang!—not a touch--he's not fond of the classics, it seems. Well, it is uncommonly dull—I'll have a rummage amongst the old lumber to pass away the time.  *        *

    *        *        *        *        *

    *        *        Here's luck!—I've discovered a fishing-rod and tackle complete; but what's the use of it here?—if I had the New River under the window I might have some sport. Oh dear! I shall never have any more sport, for I've made up my mind to starve myself to death, like that famous old fellow in the Roman History—what d'ye call him? Never mind. To make my sad end more affecting I'll write my own epitaph—something in this way—

> 'Here lies poor Francis Pickleberry,
>     Who when alive ——'

Well, what about when I was alive?

> 'Who when alive drank port and sherry.'

Port and sherry won't do!

> ——— 'Poor Francis Pickleberry,
> Who when alive drank ale and perry.'

I'm obliged to put in 'perry' for the rhyme, though we get nothing but small-beer at Doctor Drone's.

'And dearly loved ——'

Dearly loved—what was it I dearly loved?—Julia Mildmay, of course; but I'm afraid they'd laugh at me if I put it on my tomb, so I must try something else—

'And dearly loved—trap-ball and cricket.'

Bravo!

'But now he's dead—now he's dead ——'

I wish that horrid cock would leave off crowing—

'But now he's dead ——'

I'm regularly stuck for the rest of the line—

'But now he's dead ——'

Confound old Cinnamon! there he goes again! I wish every Cochin-China cock in the world was smothered—

'But now he's dead ——'

I'm getting awfully hungry; but I'll be firm—there will soon be an end to my misery—

'But now he's dead ——'

There's somebody at the door—who can it be? I'll just ask.    *    *    *    *

" It was Mary the cookmaid, who thought I might like a bit of roast lamb and an apple turnover, which she has put up in a basket, that she

says I'm to draw up from the yard to the leads outside the window.   Mary is very kind, I'm sure, and I don't like to hurt her feelings by refusing her offer, though I shan't touch a morsel of the food.   The fishing-line will do capitally to fasten to the basket and haul it up.        *        *
       *        *        *        *        *

"Mary's a trump!   I've got the basket—all right—the contents are *beautiful!*—there's a small bottle of something that smells like currant-wine; I'll taste it, to be certain.        *        *        *
It actually is currant-wine, and I'm particularly fond of it.   Mary's a love!   But I must not give way to my longings—I'll be a Spartan—I'll be a brick!   There—I've corked the bottle again, and put away the basket.   I wonder how long a boy could live without eating!   I'll have a try at my epitaph again!

"Here lies — roast lamb — no, no, I mean Francis Pickleberry—who when alive drank— currant-wine—no—apple turnover—no, no—I *do* feel so faint I must have another peep into the basket.   *        *        *        *        *
       *        *        Well,—if Mary hasn't sent a lot of pickled walnuts with the cold lamb.   Oh! —it's too much for weak human nature.        *
       *        *        *        *        *
There!—it's done: the roast lamb, the pickled walnuts, the apple turnover, and the currant-

wine, have all vanished—I feel remarkably jolly now—though I know I ought to be very sad and penitent. One, two—two o'clock !—how slowly the clocks go to-day ! Is there nothing I can do to keep myself alive ? Hollo !—I know—I'll go fishing—I ought to say fowling—for that old cinnamon cock who will persist in crowing away his voice. The fishing-rod will be long enough to reach from the leads over the wall, and the line is strong enough to bear an ostrich—so here goes!

  *   *   *   *   *

"Hurray! I've caught old Cinnamon, by making a noose at the end of the fishing-line, which I dropped quietly over his head, and hoisted up my gentleman, fluttering and kicking furiously, from a large domestic circle of hens and chickens, who witnessed the ' terrific ascent' of their respectable parent, with the utmost consternation. The alarm which old Cinnamon himself experienced on his involuntary elevation, subsided as soon as he found himself safely landed in ' The Museum,' and he is now standing opposite the noseless bust of Billy Pitt, which he is apparently criticising, with his head bent knowingly on one side, like the crabbed-faced gentlemen one sees at the Royal Academy Exhibition, who want to be thought judges of art. I dare say the poor old fellow is thinking of his wives and family, from whom he has been

so cruelly separated, so out of pure humanity I'll
see if I cannot catch some of his relatives to keep
him company       *       *

   *       *       *       *       *

" All right ! I've got the speckled Dorking hen,
who resisted with all the energy of her sex, and
made a dreadful outcry against the ascending process. Old Cinnamon is delighted to see her, and
they are clucking away at a great rate in the
corner, wondering, no doubt, where they have got
to. I'll leave them, and make another throw of
my lasso amongst the bereaved family.       *

   *       *       *       *       *

" Bravo! I've hauled up the black Spanish
pullet, with the beautiful top-knot, who seems to
be the favourite of old Cinnamon, and the rival of
the speckled beauty — who rushed at her, and
would have punished her severely but for the in-
terference of old Cinnamon, who, I should think,
has quite enough to do to keep the peace amongst
his wives. Now for the lasso, and rest of the
family. This is the jolliest sport !  *       *

   *       *       *       *       *

" I've got the lot!—Four hens and half a
dozen well-grown chicks, besides old Cinnamon.
What a beautiful family !—Only they *will* make
such a confounded crowing and clucking they'll
be heard down stairs, and then, shan't I catch it !

Hollo! there's somebody coming up.—Where's my Virgil?

"'Æneas celsa in puppi, jam certus,'—I wish I could twist old Cinnamon's neck,—it's too late, they're unlocking the door,—'jam certus,' it's the governor    *    *

     *    *      No, it's not.—It was only Martha Mims—with such good news. My aunts Flathers have come, and got my pardon from papa and mamma, and I'm to be released, and go down to dinner, and I'm never to play the wag again, and, *I never will*, because my aunts are trumps. Wasn't Martha surprised at my collection of poultry! How they got into 'the Museum,' she couldn't imagine; but she'll say nothing about it down-stairs, and I'll drop old Cinnamon and his family on the other side of the wall,—it will be such fun!    *     *

   *     * There—I've sent them all fluttering into Mrs. Smith's flower garden; and there's Bagster come into his yard, to feed the poultry, and wondering what has become of them: he puts on his spectacles, but he can't find them anywhere, and Mrs. Smith has entered her garden with her little dog, who commences an indiscriminate chase of old Cinnamon and his family amongst the flower-pots and tulips, regardless of her distracted cries; and Bagster has terrified his housekeeper into fits by shouting 'thieves,' with

all his might; and Mrs. Smith has gone into
hysterics on a bed of mignionette, and — I'm
coming, Martha, — hurray! '*Æneas celsa in
puppi*,' — tootle-too-too, tootle-ootle-ootle-too—
coming!"

# CHAPTER XIII.

A SOLEMN rejoicing was held on the evening of
Frank's liberation; but first Mr. Pickleberry took
him into his study, where he spoke to him so
seriously, and at the same time so kindly, about
his heedlessness and love of fun—or, more properly, his love of mischief,—that Frank felt
heartily ashamed of himself, and hung his head
to conceal the tears that rolled plentifully down
his cheeks. . Mr. Pickleberry, perceiving the
impression he had made upon the penitent, took
his hand tenderly.

"I would not, my dear boy," said he, "deny
you one innocent recreation, befitting your age,
that my means can compass. I know that youth
is the season of pleasure. With you, life is still
a sunny morning; fresh flowers spring in your
path, and hope beckons you in the distance.
But the time must come when the sky shall grow

dark, and the flowers wither; when the cares of the world shall tame your spirit; when age shall dim the fire of your eye, and make your light foot press heavily on the earth. Enjoy then, my child, the bright hour while it lasts; but enjoy it so that it may bring no reproach from your conscience. In your gayest moments, pause, and ask yourself if your gratification can give pain to another; if it does, forego it :—and as the boy is the father of the man, let your sports of to-day fit you for the higher and nobler duties of the future."

Frank was that evening more serious than I had ever seen him; but there was no sadness in his countenance; indeed, I thought I never saw him look so happy as when we were all sitting round the tea-table,—for I should mention that, at a private interview with Mrs. Pickleberry, she asked me to come down with the children to tea; observing at the time that, although she meant to look over what had passed, yet she must say, and she regretted having to do so—but it was better, under the circumstances, to be candid,—she must say that I had been the cause of the unpleasant occurrence that had taken place.

I believe I expressed my astonishment at this unexpected charge by a look, for Mrs. Pickleberry, with the gentlest motion of her hand and head, said :—

" You need not open your eyes so, Miss Mims, as if what I said surprised you. You'll excuse me observing that it is very disrespectful of a young person in your situation to open her eyes in that manner, especially when I am alluding, in the most delicate manner possible, to—to—a—dear me, what was it I was alluding to?"

" You said, madam, that I was the cause of the disagreeable occurrence that had taken place. If you would only have the goodness to point out how——"

" Really, Miss Mims, I don't understand being cross-examined and flown at in this way; I suppose I am at liberty to make a simple remark in my own house without being called to account for it. Now *pray* don't interrupt me, for my nerves are so shattered, I cannot bear the violence of your temper. You had better retire to the nursery; and when you have composed yourself, I shall be glad if you will have the goodness to make the children neat—though I dare say you'll pay no attention to what I say—and, if you have no particular engagement yourself this evening, will you do me the favour to accompany them down to tea?"

I made no reply to this stinging speech but a low curtsey; and, rushing out of the room, ran upstairs to my bedroom, where I could give way to my feelings, after which I felt better; and, having dressed the children, we marched down to the parlour, where the other members of the family were assembled.

The evening commenced rather stiffly, for the younger children were evidently awe-struck by the sight of the hissing tea-urn on the table; and being duly impressed by me with the necessity for showing papa and mamma how polite we could be when we pleased, kept themselves as quiet as mice until Mr. Pickleberry broke the ice by taking Arabella on his knee, and telling her a very wonderful story about a certain little woman who resided in a shoe, and had such a numerous family of children that she was greatly embarrassed what to do with them all. This was followed by a very curious and ancient song about a sixpence, which was in some way connected with a bag full of the grain called rye, and in which mention was made of a very singular pie, composed of twenty-four blackbirds, baked especially for his majesty's eating, who was greatly surprised, on cutting open the said pie with a view to dining thereon, to hear the blackbirds all singing together, like the chorus in the oratorios at Exeter Hall. The merriment which these legends created amongst the little folks quite destroyed the character for the decorum of the nursery which I had hoped we should have gained on the occasion. Indeed, the more I nudged them privately, and exhorted them by masonic looks and signs to sit quiet, the more the worrying little creatures laughed and talked, and conducted themselves so outrageously, that I feared we should all be condemned to ignominious banishment. Mr. Pickleberry, however, seemed to encourage their tumultuous proceedings, and requested me, when I wished to interfere, to " let the poor things enjoy themselves," and actually promoted the uproar by flinging a handful of sugar-plums and almonds on the carpet for them to scramble for. I really feel myself unable to describe the scene that ensued. Mr. Pickleberry laughed immoderately; and Mrs. Pickleberry, who was seized with an unusually amiable fit that evening, condescended to smile faintly once or twice, and never made the slightest allusion to her nervous headache. The Misses Flathers—who had got Frank between them, and were industriously stuffing him with plum-cake and macaroons—being strong advocates for unlimited play and universal freedom for children, were perfectly happy at the riot. Theodore Tunks the speckled page, who had been the picture of misery ever since Frank's disappearance, was literally beside himself with joy, and gave vent to his feelings in continual explosions of unprovoked laughter, and the involuntary performance of a polka-step while handing round the muffins.

After tea we had a little concert, Miss Flathers

presiding at the piano, and performing, as on former occasions, the overture to *Tancredi* with great manual energy.

Miss Hannah Flathers, who was reported to have had a sweet little voice about the period of the battle of Waterloo, was induced, as there were no strangers present, to try *The Banks of Allan Water;* but I regret I was at too great a distance from the vocalist (quite on the other side of the room) to hear a note of the song, which appeared to be rather of a confidential nature than other-wise. Then we had, by special desire, a Dutch concert, in which all the children sang toge-ther what song each liked best, while Miss Flathers played the overture to *Tancredi* on the piano as an accompaniment. The effect was in the highest degree stunning, especially when Bijou joined in with a dismal howl. The success was indeed complete, and so pleased were the performers with their individual exertions, that it required the exercise of strong parental autho-rity before silence could be restored, and the vocal corps dismissed with kisses and sugar-plums to the nursery.

The serenity we enjoyed for some days after this solemn peace-making was truly delightful. Frank appeared to be completely reformed—or nearly so; for, with the exception of blacking his face and hands, and those of Georgina, Maria, and Arabella, with burnt cork, for the purpose of giving me an Ethiopian serenade, nothing could be more correct and orderly than his conduct. The mess, though, those children were in I shall never forget,—nor, I dare say, will little Alf,—who nearly went into fits, when he saw the four black performers march into the nursery. I must admit, however, that Frank did the " bones" surprisingly; and Georgina's execution on a wooden hoop, with a piece of stiff brown paper tied over it for a tambourine, was really wonderful for her age.

At other times, Frank used to read aloud for us in the nursery—*The Swiss Family Robinson—The Travels of Rolando*, and other books of the same character; for he took an intense delight, as most boys do, in exciting narratives of wild adventures on the wide ocean, or the untrodden desert.

The holidays were now drawing to a close; but before Frank's return to school, he obtained permission from his papa to have one day's fishing on the Lea with Egerton Paley, who was never known to get into any kind of mischief. Mr. Pickleberry's long-neglected fishing-rod was therefore taken out of " The Museum," carefully cleaned, and fitted up for service. Frank and Theodore Tunks held serious consultations respecting the selection of lines, floats, and hooks,

and the attractiveness of minnows, gentles, and
lob-worms for perch, dace, and tench.    Tunks,
to his immense delight, was allowed to attend the
young anglers with a capacious covered basket,
for the double purpose of carrying out a large
stock of bread and meat for the party, and of
containing the enormous quantity of fish they
meant to bring home.    That night Egerton Paley
slept with Frank, in order that they might be
ready for a timely start.

It was still young morning when I heard them
moving about; and presently the sound of descending footsteps on the stairs apprised me that
the trio were about to sally forth.    I got up,
and looked out at the window.    Phœbus, as the
poets say, had left "a burning kiss on Thetis'
cheek," and mounted his chariot in the East;—
which makes me conclude that Phœbus was an early
'bus man, living in Whitechapel.    Brown-coated
sparrows twittered and chattered amongst the
shrubs in the square; greengrocers, and butchers'
boys, with fast-trotting ponies and light carts, railway vans, and lumbering reservoirs—invented for
the suppression of dust—had begun to make their
appearance in the streets.    Not a cloud was in the
sky; and the morning—as the tea-dealers elo-
quently observe, when expatiating upon the supe-
riority of their fine hyson-flavoured Pekoe—was
one that "might fearlessly defy competition."

I saw the two boys crossing the square with their fishing-rods on their shoulder, and could hear their merry laugh ringing through the silent street, as they bounded rather than walked along in the freshness of youth and life and anticipated pleasure. The speckled page followed, carrying the basket for the spoil, and scarcely less excited than Frank and Egerton at the idea of their day's sport. I looked after them until they turned into the next street, when, as it was only five o'clock, I crept into bed again, and had a comfortable nap till seven.

The adventures of the fishing-party during that day I afterwards collected from what the newspapers call an "authentic source," so that I can vouch for their accuracy.

Directing their course to the well-known "Angel" at Islington, the boys got into the New Road, somewhere near the Regent's Park, from whence they hurried onward, without so much as stopping to admire those famous wayside studios, with their groups of muscular angels, and Apollos, and chubby Cupids and Graces, which Mr. O'Leary, the "Special Correspondent" of the *Tipperary Flagellator*, says are the born images of those that poor Tyrone Power used to sing about in *The Groves of Blarney*—

> "There are statues gracin'
> This noble place in ;
> All heathen goddesses and gods so fair ;

Bould Neptune, Plutarch,
And Nicodemus,
All standing naked in the open air."

The young excursionists, fresh and active as
deer, breasted the hill at Pentonville gallantly,
and turning to the left at the " Angel," pushed on
without halting till they saw the " winding Lea "
meandering through the flat pastures and meadows
that lie between Lea-bridge and Walthamstow.
They had already obtained the necessary permission
to fish the preserved waters, in the vicinity of the
"Horse and Groom,"—a little hostelrie dear to the
followers of old Izaak Walton, where the stuffed
remains of many a carp, tench, and chubb, of
enormous size and weight—captured perhaps in
those remote ages when the giant sons of Anak
walked the earth, and the finny tribes of the Lea
were proportionate in their dimensions—were en-
shrined in glass cases, and hung round the parlour,
with wonderful legends attached, that made the
piscatorial pigmies of Cockaigne blush with very
shame at the smallness of the modern race of
gudgeons. The rods and tackle were speedily
put in order, and the most tempting bait selected
to begin with. Intense was the anxiety of the young
fishermen as they watched their floats stealing slowly
down the stream; and if a slight ripple agitated
one of them ever so little, or a stray weed clinging
to their line caused it to strain, how the heart of

the angler would throb, in the hope that it might
be—a nibble! A couple of hours, however, passed
in this manner with no visible results, except a
few skeins of slimy river-grass, made the sport
appear rather monotonous to Frank, who cast his
line impatiently here and there, until at last he
got his hook entangled in the tall sedges that
grew near the shore. Egerton, perceiving his
embarrassment, hastened to his assistance, and
reaching forward to lay hold of the line, lost his
balance and fell into the river, which at that
spot was deep and rapid. A sullen dash of waters
—a piercing shriek—a wild tossing of the hands
for a few moments—and then—the dull stream
closed over the struggling boy. Paralysed at the
sight, Frank stood for some seconds gazing in
mute horror on his companion as he disappeared,
while Tunks, who had been engaged in a curious
investigation of the ham sandwiches in the basket,
set up a loud and piteous howl, that might have
startled the water nymphs, if any of these classic
beings haunted the oozy banks of the Lea. The
natural energy and courage of Frank's nature
did not, however, long desert him, and by the
time the pale face of his playmate again rose to
the surface of the water, with fearful eyes,—and
a faint gurgling cry for help reached his ear, he
had divested himself of his shoes and jacket, and
calling to Egerton to "strike out" and "not to

be afraid," he sprang from the bank, and being a
bold and active swimmer, reached the drowning
boy in a few strokes, and caught his hand as he
was going down for the second time. The instinct
of self-preservation caused Egerton to cling desperately to Frank, who vainly endeavoured to loose
the rigid fingers that clasped his neck. In vain
he called to him to let go his hold, or they must
both be drowned; the poor boy was unconscious
of everything save the presence of some object,
which he grappled with death-like tenacity. Rendered almost powerless by the manner in which
Egerton clung to him, Frank felt that he could
not support his burthen many minutes longer;—
his strength was fast failing him, and his weary
arms had ceased to move,—the rippling waters rose
to his mouth, and stopped his thick-coming breath;
—a dark veil seemed to blot the blue sky, and a
roaring as of a thousand cataracts filled his ears;—
then came thoughts of home,—his beloved parents
and his little sisters, whom he should never see
again. Poor Frank! Was he to perish thus?
No. Providence watched over him, and sent him
succour in his extremity. An elderly gentleman,
accompanied by a fine Newfoundland dog, was
taking an early walk by the river side, when, hearing
the cries of the page, he hastened to the spot,
and perceiving the perilous situation of the boys,
called to his dog to " go in and fetch 'em." The

sagacious animal, comprehending his duty, instantly plunged into the river, and seizing Frank's shoulder, supported him and the now senseless Egerton to the bank, upon which they were dragged by the aid of some labourers, who had also been drawn by Theodore's cries to the place. By these people the two boys were carried to the fishing-station, where they were placed in warm beds, and received all the attention and care their state demanded.

# CHAPTER XIV.

The Young Patient—Frank Watching by the Bedside of Egerton
—The Widow's Story—A Joyful Meeting—And a Farewell
*Soirée,* which brings the indulgent Reader to the Close of the
Holidays, and the Departure of Frank and his friend Egerton
for Dr. Drone's Establishment.

A MESSENGER had been despatched, in the course
of the day, to Frank's parents by the doctor who
had been called in, informing them of the alarming accident that had befallen the two boys.
Frank, who had not been so long in the water,
nor had suffered so much by exhaustion as Egerton,
who was a weak delicate boy, speedily recovered,
and after having partaken of some mulled wine,
and enjoyed a couple of hours' refreshing sleep,
was permitted by the doctor to put on his
clothes, which had been thoroughly dried at the
kitchen fire, and to sit by the bed of Egerton,
who being still weak, was ordered to be kept very
quiet. Stealing on tip-toe into the darkened room,
Frank moved silently to the bedside of his friend,
who lay so still that he fancied he was asleep,
until he heard him pronounce his name softly,—

"Frank; is it *you*?"

"Yes, Egerton; but we must not speak until you get a little stronger—the doctor says so."

"I know—I know; but tell me, has my poor mother heard what has happened, does she know that I am safe?"

"The people here have sent word home, and they'll be sure to let your mother know; so make your mind easy, and try and sleep—there's a good fellow."

"I will—I will; but sit down there by the bedside, Frank; now give me your hand. There, that will do. You saved my life, Frank, didn't you?—I thought when I sank that I saw your face looking down on me through the waters,—but it seemed so far off,—and when I thought to reach it, it floated away,—and I heard mother's voice singing,—oh! such a sweet faint song——"

"Hush, Egerton, hush! or I must leave you."

"Well, I'll speak no more;" and with his pale face turned towards Frank, whose hand he still grasped, he continued to gaze on the features of his friend, until he sank into a profound and peaceful sleep.

It was a beautiful and purifying sight to behold those two warm-hearted boys clinging one to another, unprompted by the mean or selfish motives that form too often the bond of our friendships in riper age. In their young and generous **hearts** there was no secret thought of benefits to be received or rendered; no worldly calculations by which their affections **were to be** weighed and measured to the best advantage, like a marketable commodity. There **is** nothing **that** gives me greater pleasure to see than those early attachments; and I often think we do not sufficiently cherish in after life our school friendships, formed at a period when the heart is susceptible of the **best** and purest impressions.

The mother of Egerton Paley was **the widow of** an officer who had died in **India.** Married against the consent of his friends, Captain Paley carried his young wife with him to India when, a few months after their marriage, his regiment was ordered to the East. During six years they enjoyed uninterrupted happiness; one child blessed their union, but so delicate was the tender blossom, the physicians agreed in opinion that nothing could preserve the infant's **life** if it was not immediately sent to Europe. To save the life of their darling, the doting parents resolved then to sacrifice their own feelings, and it was determined that Mrs. Paley and little **Egerton** should proceed directly to England, to be followed **by** Captain Paley the following year, when he hoped to obtain leave of absence. Alas for human hopes! he never lived to behold again those dear objects of his love: a malignant fever had carried him off a

few days before the time fixed for his departure
from India; and the ship that should have brought
him to the arms of his wife, conveyed her the
afflicting intelligence of his death. Deprived of
a husband to whom she was tenderly attached,
the poor widow's existence became absorbed in
her boy, who requited her love with all the
warmth of an affectionate heart.

At school Frank and Egerton first met, and
notwithstanding the dissimilarity of their characters in some respects—the energetic and impulsive
disposition of the one being strikingly contrasted
with the thoughtful and gentle nature of the
other—they became constant companions and fast
friends; Frank thrashing any boy of his class
who attempted to bully his *protégé*, and Egerton
helping his friend with his lessons when, as it
sometimes happened, a novel or a newspaper was
taken by mistake for Virgil or Euclid in the hours
for study.

To return:—early in the afternoon a carriage
drove up to the " Horse and Groom," and Mr. and
Mrs. Pickleberry and Mrs. Paley descending from it,
were instantly conducted by a servant to Egerton's
bedroom. They entered the chamber cautiously,
for the wearied boy still slept, with his hand
clasped in that of Frank, who, perceiving his
father and mother, sprang from his seat and threw
himself into their arms. The withdrawal of

Frank's hand, though done as gently as possible, aroused Egerton, who gazed inquiringly at his visitors, unable to recognise them, until he felt his mother's lips pressed to his, her warm tears falling on his brow, and her gentle voice murmuring, through the sobs that almost choked her utterance, blessings and thanksgivings to the Almighty Power that had preserved her child. A thrilling exclamation of joy burst from Egerton as, winding his arms around his mother's neck, he, for some minutes, felt that fulness of joy for which words have no adequate expression. When he had become somewhat composed, he called to Frank—who was regarded as a perfect hero, by all who had heard of his intrepidity in exposing his own life to save that of his companion, who, but for his assistance, would inevitably have been drowned.

Mrs. Paley could, therefore, not sufficiently express her gratitude to Frank, whom she embraced over and over again, calling him her brave, her noble boy, the preserver of her dear child, and a thousand other endearing expressions which may be easily imagined.

Not to prolong this scene, which was deeply affecting to all parties—even Mrs. Pickleberry forgot her nerves and her feelings, and shed tears of real happiness as she pressed her son to her heart,—it may suffice to say, that Egerton was sufficiently recovered to be removed on the fol-

lowing morning to Mr. Pickleberry's, where he
and his mother had been invited to spend the few
days which remained of the vacation, after which
the boys were to return to Dr. Drone's scholastic
establishment at Brighton.

These intervening days were passed so quietly,
that I do not remember any occurrence of suffi-
cient importance to be worth recording, except a
little farewell *soirée*—quite a domestic affair—
which was given by the young ladies to Frank
and Egerton, who received a hint at the same
time that their company would be more accept-
able if they brought a good lot of jumballs and
almond-cakes in their pockets to the party.

In compliment to the visitors, Georgina brought
forward the Lilliputian tea-service, presented to
her on her eighth birthday by her aunt Miss
Flathers, and made tea in the real China teapot
attached to the set. The entertainment was what
they call very *recherché*—mugs and pinafores were
entirely excluded; and all the dolls, who had
been dressed in their gayest attire, were allowed
to sit on the chimney-piece, from whence, like the
ladies in the gallery at a lord mayor's dinner, they
could behold the festivities, if they could not par-
ticipate in them. The currant-cake, made by
Mary the cook, gave, I am happy to say, universal
satisfaction; especially when it was known that
another cake of similar manufacture, only three

times as big, had been packed up, with a great
variety of confectionery, in Frank's box, which
he was to take back to school. I am afraid it
reached the dreadful hour of ten o'clock before we
thought of breaking up and retiring to bed. How
the boys slept that night I cannot tell; but at the
awful hour of twelve, "when churchyards yawn"
and graves give up their ghosts, a figure clad
all in white—Miss Hannah Flathers, in fact, in
her night costume—was seen gliding noiselessly
into Frank's bedroom. What she wanted there
I really cannot tell, but I believe that Frank found
next morning, in his trowsers pocket, a neat little
*porte monnaie*, containing a new sovereign, which
he had no recollection of being there on going to
bed.

The following morning, about seven o'clock,
there was an unusual bustle in the house; and
Theodore Tunks, the speckled page, was busily
engaged thrusting a collection of trunks and boxes,
and cricket-bats, and basket-sticks into a cab
which stood at the door, to convey the boys to the
London-bridge Railway Station. Mary the cookmaid, Sarah the housemaid, and Annette the lady's
maid, were clustered together on the area steps—
reminding one, as they stood embracing and embraced, of the statues of the "Three Graces."
Not so elegant, perhaps, though certainly better

provided with clothing than the classical ladies. They were waiting to have a parting look and a kind word from Master Frank before he quitted us. As I also wanted to bid him "good-bye," I planted myself on the landing, and met him coming from his mother's room, where he had been taking leave of her.

" Good-bye, Frank; I'm sorry you are leaving us," said I, offering to shake hands with him.

Looking in my face with a comical expression, in which there was as much of drollery as penitence, he said :—

" You ought to be glad to get rid of me, Martha, for I have been a sad plague to you since I've been home; but, never mind, I shall be a bigger and a better boy, when I come back next vacation, and then I'll play no more practical jokes ; so you'll forgive me, Martha, won't you ?"

I had only time to kiss the dear boy, and assure him that I had never been really angry with him; when his father, who was waiting in the hall, called to him to make haste. Obeying the summons, he ran downstairs and jumped into the cab with his father and Egerton. As the vehicle turned the corner, the three kitchen graces in the area thrust the corners of their aprons into their respective right eyes; Tunks, the speckled page, rushed down into the scullery to conceal his emotion; while I returned to the nursery to add this last incident to my narrative of FRANK PICKLEBERRY'S HOLIDAYS, AND HOW THEY WERE SPENT.

PRINTED BY COX (BROS.) AND WYMAN, GREAT QUEEN STREET.

# List of the Novels and Tales

OF

## SIR EDWARD BULWER LYTTON, BART.

## Pelham.

1s. 6d. Railway Library. Large Edition, cloth gilt, 3s. 6d.

" PELHAM " is at once the most finished as a narrative, the most vigorous in execution, and taking its exuberant wit and daring originality into account, it must be considered as the most decided indication of what is rather felt than defined by the word *genius*.

## Paul Clifford.

1s. 6d. Railway Library. Large Edition, cloth gilt, 3s. 6d.

" PAUL CLIFFORD " is a work *sui generis*. It is a political and social satire worked out through the gravest agencies;—in form, a burlesque—in essentials, a tragedy.

## Eugene Aram.

1s. 6d. Railway Library. Large Edition, cloth gilt, 3s. 6d.

" EUGENE ARAM " attests an immense progress in the resources of art in fiction; it grasps the materials of terror and pity with a master's hand, and connects them with all the gradual progress of the drama, into tragic completeness.

## The Last Days of Pompeii.

1s. 6d. Railway Library. Large Edition, cloth gilt, 3s. 6d.

The plot commencing lightly with the gay descriptions of idle life, its baths and its banquets, deepens gradually towards the awful magnificence of the catastrophe. All our passions are alternately " rocked as on a music scale " by the scene in the gladiatorial arena,—the inhuman delight of the spectators,—the first outburst of the irruption from the Mount of Fire,—the phenomena of the general destruction, —to the still unnoticed disappearance of Nydia, under the smile of awaking Dawn.

## Ernest Maltravers.

1s. 6d. Railway Library. Large Edition, cloth gilt, 3s. 6d.

# Rienzi.

1s. 6d. Railway Library.   Large Edition, cloth gilt, **3s. 6d.**

The early middle age of Italy rises before us; rude, yet struggling into light, **and** seeking escape into civilization by **return to** the classic past; the grand soul of the "Last Tribune" **comes to** recall again, **for a** momentary interval, the majesty of antique Rome, startling, **as** with the ghost of the classic giantess, the barbarian courts of the victor North.   Rienzi himself is the master-spirit of the whole.

# Alice; or, the Mysteries.

1s. 6d. Railway Library.   Large Edition, cloth gilt, 3s. 6d.

The typical **intentions** are with admirable art kept **so far** subordinate **to the** story, that we always feel ourselves in the company of living agents; and **it** is only when our interest in the events of the tale and the destinies of its leading characters is fully satisfied, that we pause **to** look back at the secret philosophy that pervades the narrative, and **become** sensible **of the wisdom we** have acquired in the pleasure we **have** received.

# Night and Morning.

1s. 6d. Railway Library.   Large Edition, cloth gilt, 4s.

" NIGHT AND MORNING " is the most generally popular of the author's works; its materials are of a homelier and coarser kind than many of them; but their texture is strong and their hues brilliant. And in proportion as the work dispenses with the more reflective beauties that distinguish " MALTRAVERS," it gains as an animated **and** powerful story of human life.

# The Pilgrims of the Rhine.

1s. Railway Library.   Large Edition, cloth gilt, **2s. 6d.**

The loveliest and most fanciful of this varied catalogue of fiction.   It gathers together, as into a garland of flowers, the associations, the history, the legends, the romance of the Rhine.   Nothing like it, for **the** comprehension of the poetical aspects of places hallowed by tradition, exists **in** our language; and its originality **is so toned down into** familiar sweetness, that it is scarcely detected till **we search for some** work with which to compare it, and—find none.

## ROUTLEDGE'S USEFUL LIBRARY.

*Price One Shilling each, unless specified.*

1 A Ladies' **and** Gentlemen's Letter-Writer.
2 Household Economy; or, Domestic Hints for Persons of Moderate Income. *Anne Bowman.*
3 Landmarks **of the** History of England (1s. 6d.) *Rev. James White.*
4 Landmarks of the History of Greece, with **a** Map (1s. 6d.) *Rev. J. White.*
5 **Common** Things of Every-Day Life. *Anne Bowman.*
6 Martin Doyle's Things worth Knowing, a Book of General Practical Utility.
7 Landlord and Tenant (The Law of), with **an** Appendix of Useful Forms, Glossary of Law Terms. *W. A. Holdsworth.*
8 Lives of Good Servants. *Author of " Mary Powell."*
9 History of France, from the Earliest Period to the Peace of Paris, 1856. *Amelia Edwards.*
10 Wills, Executors, and Administrators (The Law of), with Useful Forms. *W. A. Holdsworth.*
11 Rundell's Domestic Cookery, unabridged, with Illustrations.
12 The Tricks of Trade, in the Adulterations of Food and Physic. *Revised and Edited by Dr. Nuttall.*
13 Notes on Health: How to Preserve or Regain it. *W. T. Coleman, M.D.*
14 Novelties, Inventions, and Discoveries in Art, Science, and Manufactures (1s. 6d.) *George Dodd.*
15 Common Objects of the Microscope, with 400 Illustrations. *Rev. J. G. Wood.*
16 Law of Bankruptcy. *W. A. Holdsworth.*
17 One Thousand Hints for the Table, including Wines.
18 How to Make Money; a Practical Treatise on Business. *E. T. Freedley.*
19 Household Law, or the Rights and Wrongs of Men and Women (2s.) *Fonblanque.*

## BOOKS FOR THE COUNTRY.

*Price One Shilling per Volume, unless specified.*

In limp cloth Covers or Ornamental Boards, with Illustrations.

1 Angling, and Where to Go. *R. Blakey.*
2 Pigeons and Rabbits. *Delamer.*
3 Shooting. *Blakey.*
4 The Sheep. *Martin.*
5 Flax and Hemp. *Delamer.*
6 The Poultry Yard. *Watts.*
7 The Pig. *Martin and Sidney*
8 Cattle (1s. 6d.) *Martin and Raynbird.*
10 The Horse. *Cecil and Youatt.*
11 Bees. *Rev. J. G. Wood.*
12 Cage and Singing Birds. *H. G. Adams.*
13 Small Farms. *M. Doyle.*
14 The Kitchen Garden. *Delamer.*
15 The Flower Garden. *Delamer.*
16 Rural Economy. *M. Doyle.*
17 Farm and Garden Produce. *M. Doyle.*
18 Common Objects of the Sea Shore. *Rev. J. G. Wood.*
19 Common Objects of the Country. *Rev. J. G. Wood.*
20 Agricultural Chemistry (1s. 6d.) *Sibson and Voelcker.*
21 Woodlands, Heaths, and Hedges. *Coleman.*
22 British Ferns, illustrated by W. S. Coleman. *Thomas Moore, F.L.S.*
23 Favourite Flowers: How to Grow them. *A. G. Sutton.*
24 British Butterflies. *W. S. Coleman.*
25 The Rat, its History, with Anecdotes by Uncle James (1s. 6d.)
26 Dogs, their Management, &c. (1s. 6d.) *Edward Mayhew.*
27 Hints for Farmers. *R. Scott Burn.*
28 British Birds' Eggs and Nests. *Rev. J. C. Atkinson.*
29 British Timber Trees (1s. 6d.) *Blenkarn.*
30 Wild Flowers (2s.) *Spencer Thomson.*

## ROUTLEDGE'S HOUSEHOLD MANUALS.

*Fcap. 8vo, price Sixpence each, cloth limp.*

1 THE COOK'S OWN BOOK; a Manual of Cookery for the Kitchen and the Cottage. By GEORGIANA HILL. With Practical Illustrations.

2 THE LADY'S LETTER WRITER. } With Applications for Situations, Forms of Address to
3 THE GENTLEMAN'S LETTER WRITER. } Persons of Title, &c.

4 VILLAGE MUSEUM; or, How we Gathered Profit with Pleasure. By Rev. G. T. HOARE.

# BY CAPTAIN MARRYAT.

Price 2s. each, boards; or 2s. 6d. cloth gilt.

MIDSHIPMAN EASY.
PETER SIMPLE.
KING'S OWN.
RATTLIN THE REEFER. (Edited.)
JACOB FAITHFUL.
JAPHET IN SEARCH OF A FATHER.
PACHA OF MANY TALES.

VALERIE.
NEWTON FORSTER.
DOG FIEND; or, Snarley-yow.
POACHER.
PHANTOM SHIP.
PERCIVAL KEENE.
FRANK MILDMAY.

# BY THE RIGHT HON. B. DISRAELI.

Price 1s. 6d. each, boards.

THE YOUNG DUKE.
TANCRED.
VENETIA.
CONTARINI FLEMING.

CONINGSBY.
SYBIL.
ALROY.
IXION.

Price 2s. each, boards; or, in cloth, 2s. 6d.

HENRIETTA TEMPLE.

VIVIAN GREY.

# BY J. F. COOPER.

In fcap. 8vo, price Eighteenpence each, boards; or, in cloth, 2s.

LAST OF THE MOHICANS.
SPY.
LIONEL LINCOLN.
PILOT.
PIONEERS.
SEA LIONS.
BORDERERS, or Heathcotes.
BRAVO.
HOMEWARD BOUND.
AFLOAT AND ASHORE.
SATANSTOE.
WYANDOTTE.
MARK'S REEF.

DEERSLAYER.
OAK OPENINGS.
PATHFINDER.
HEADSMAN.
WATER WITCH.
TWO ADMIRALS.
MILES WALLINGFORD.
PRAIRIE.
RED ROVER.
EVE EFFINGHAM.
HEIDENMAUER.
PRECAUTION.
JACK TIER.

# BY W. H. AINSWORTH.

Price 1s. 6d. each, boards.

MISER'S DAUGHTER.
GUY FAWKES.
SPENDTHRIFT.
WINDSOR CASTLE.

CRICHTON.
ROOKWOOD.
STAR CHAMBER.

Price 2s. each, boards; or in cloth gilt, 2s. 6d.

TOWER OF LONDON.
OLD ST. PAUL'S.
LANCASHIRE WITCHES.

MERVYN CLITHEROE.
FLITCH OF BACON.
OVINGDEAN GRANGE.

BALLADS, Illustrated.

# BY FREDERICK GERSTAECKER.

In fcap. 8vo, price 1s. 6d. each, boards.

WILD SPORTS OF THE FAR WEST.

PIRATES OF THE MISSISSIPPI.

Price 2s. boards, or cl. 2s. 6d.

TWO CONVICTS.
FEATHERED ARROW.

EACH FOR HIMSELF.
A WIFE TO ORDER.

Price 1s. boards,
A SAILOR'S ADVENTURES.

## BY G. P. R. JAMES.

Price 1s., boards.

MARGARET GRAHAM.

Price 1s. 6d. each, boards.

| | |
|---|---|
| AGINCOURT. | HEIDELBERG. |
| ARABELLA STUART. | JACQUERIE. |
| ARRAH NEIL. | KING'S HIGHWAY. |
| ATTILA. | MAN-AT-ARMS. |
| BEAUCHAMP. | MARY OF BURGUNDY. |
| CASTELNEAU. | MY AUNT PONTYPOOL. |
| CASTLE OF EHRENSTEIN. | ONE IN A THOUSAND. |
| CHARLES TYRRELL. | ROBBER. |
| DELAWARE. | ROSE D'ALBRET. |
| DE L'ORME. | RUSSELL. |
| FALSE HEIR. | SIR THEODORE BROUGHTON. |
| FOREST DAYS. | STEPMOTHER. |
| FORGERY. | WHIM AND ITS CONSEQUENCES. |
| GENTLEMAN OF THE OLD SCHOOL. | DARK SCENES OF HISTORY. |

Price 2s. each, boards; or, in cloth gilt, 2s. 6d.

| | |
|---|---|
| BRIGAND. | HENRY MASTERTON. |
| CONVICT. | HENRY OF GUISE. |
| DARNLEY. | HUGUENOT. |
| GIPSY. | JOHN MARSTON HALL. |
| GOWRIE. | PHILIP AUGUSTUS. |
| MORLEY ERNSTEIN. | SMUGGLER. |
| RICHELIEU. | WOODMAN. |
| BLACK EAGLE. | |

## BY JAMES GRANT.

Price 2s. each, or 2s. 6d. cloth.

| | |
|---|---|
| MARY OF LORRAINE. | PHILIP ROLLO. |
| LEGENDS OF THE BLACK WATCH. | FRANK HILTON. |
| ARTHUR BLANE. | THE YELLOW FRIGATE. |
| HIGHLANDERS OF GLEN ORA. | HENRY OGILVIE. |
| THE ROMANCE OF WAR. | JANE SETON. |
| THE AIDE-DE-CAMP. | BOTHWELL; or, The Days of |
| SCOTTISH CAVALIER. | Mary Queen of Scots. |
| LUCY ARDEN. | OLIVER ELLIS. |

## BY W. H. MAXWELL.

Price 1s. 6d. each, boards.

| | |
|---|---|
| CAPTAIN O'SULLIVAN. | FLOOD AND FIELD. |
| WILD SPORTS OF THE WEST. | |

Price 2s. each, boards; or in cloth gilt, 2s. 6d.

| | |
|---|---|
| STORIES OF WATERLOO. | HECTOR O'HALLORAN. |
| LUCK IS EVERYTHING. | CAPTAIN BLAKE; or, My Life. |
| THE BIVOUAC. | |

## By the Author of "WHITEFRIARS."

In fcap. 8vo, price 2s. each, boards; or in cloth gilt, 2s. 6d.

| | |
|---|---|
| WHITEFRIARS; or, The Days of | WHITEHALL; or, The Days of |
| Charles II. | Charles I. |
| THE MAID OF ORLEANS. | CÆSAR BORGIA. |
| WESTMINSTER ABBEY. | OWEN TUDOR. |

Price 1s. 6d. boards.

THE GOLD WORSHIPPERS.

# RAILWAY AND SEA-SIDE READING.

## NEW VOLUMES, WITH FANCY COVERS.

Cecil; or, the Adventures of a Coxcomb. Mrs. Gore. 2s.

Garibaldi's Autobiography. By Dumas. 2s.

Wild Sports of the West. By Maxwell. 1s. 6d.

Life of a Sailor. By Captain Chamier. 2s.

Mary of Lorraine. By James Grant. 2s.

Doctor Basilius. By Dumas. 2s.

Maxwell. By Theodore Hook. 2s.

Gilbert Gurney. By Theodore Hook. 2s.

A Wife to Order. By Gerstaeker. 2s.

The Squire. By Miss Pickering. 2s.

Twenty Years of an African Slaver. By Mayer. 1s. 6d.

Love. By Lady C. Bury. 1s. 6d.

The Lost Ship. By the Author of " Cavendish." 2s.

Cozy-Nook Tales. By W. Glib. 1s.

Catherine (a Tale). By Jules Sandeau. 1s.

Comic Sketch-Book. By John Poole. 2s.

Dottings of a Lounger. By Frank Fowler. 1s.

Irving's Life and Voyages of Columbus. 2s.

The War-Lock. By the Old Sailor. 1s. 6d.

Land and Sea Tales. By the Old Sailor. 1s. 6d.

*** A List of upwards of 700 Volumes, comprising Novels or Tales by almost every Author of Note, can be had, gratis, on application to the Publishers.

LONDON: ROUTLEDGE, WARNE, AND ROUTLEDGE, FARRINGDON STREET.